Where dreams are stitched…patch by patch!

Welcome to the Blind Stitch quilt shop!
On Main Street, in the small town of Kerry Springs,
this is a haven where women, young and old,
gather to work on their quilts and to share their
hopes and dreams….

And they have much to wish for, because Kerry
Springs is home to some of the most deliciously
brooding heroes in the whole of Texas State!

Open one of Patricia Thayer's stories to enjoy the
warmth of a very special town and the strength of
old-fashioned community spirit. Best of all,
watch as Kerry Springs's singletons find the love
that they deserve….

Don't miss any of the books in this series:

Dear Reader,

Welcome back to Texas. I can't tell you how excited I am about starting The Quilt Shop in Kerry Springs series. It is centered around the The Blind Stitch quilt shop on Main Street, and the women, young and old, who gather there at the corner table to work on their quilts and share their hopes and dreams.

In the first story, *Little Cowgirl Needs a Mom,* Jenny Collins moves to Kerry Springs to manage The Blind Stitch. One day, she puts a sign in the window for a beginner's class and her first student is eight-year-old Gracie Rafferty, who wants to work on a quilt she and her mother started before her death. Jenny soon learns Gracie's mother made her daughter promise that she'd finish it. The little girl took it to heart.

That brings good-looking rancher/vineyard owner Evan Rafferty into the shop, but he refuses any help or ideas from his daughter's new friend. Of course, that doesn't stop Jenny, even if that means butting heads and risking her heart to a stubborn man who clearly doesn't want to share his.

There are so many wonderful characters in this small Texas town, I couldn't wait to tell this story.

Hope you enjoy it, too.

Patricia Thayer

PATRICIA THAYER
Little Cowgirl Needs a Mom

The Quilt Shop
in
KERRY
SPRINGS

TORONTO NEW YORK LONDON
AMSTERDAM PARIS SYDNEY HAMBURG
STOCKHOLM ATHENS TOKYO MILAN MADRID
PRAGUE WARSAW BUDAPEST AUCKLAND

ISBN-13: 978-0-373-74114-4

LITTLE COWGIRL NEEDS A MOM

First North American Publication 2011

Copyright © 2011 by Patricia Thayer

www.Harlequin.com

Printed in U.S.A..

Originally born and raised in Muncie, Indiana, **Patricia Thayer** is the second of eight children. She attended Ball State University, and soon afterward headed West. Over the years, she's made frequent visits back to the Midwest, trying to keep up with her growing family.

Patricia has called Orange County, California, home for many years. She not only enjoys the warm climate, but also the company and support of other published authors in the local writers' organization. For the past eighteen years, she has had the unwavering support and encouragement of her critique group. It's a sisterhood like no other.

When not working on a story, you might find her traveling the United States and Europe, taking in the scenery and doing story research, while thoroughly enjoying herself and the company of Steve, her husband for more than thirty-five years. Together, they have three grown sons and four grandsons. As she calls them, her own true-life heroes. On rare days off from writing, you might catch her at Disneyland, spoiling those grandkids rotten! She also volunteers for the Grandparent Autism Network.

Patricia has written for over twenty years and has authored more than thirty-six books for Silhouette Books and Harlequin Mills & Boon. She has been nominated for both the National Readers' Choice Award and the prestigious RITA® Award. Her book *Nothing Short of a Miracle* won an *RT Book Reviews* Choice award.

A longtime member of Romance Writers of America, she has served as president and held many other board positions for her local chapter in Orange County. She's a firm believer in giving back.

Check her website at www.patriciathayer.com for upcoming books.

To Harrison John,
your smiles melt my heart.

And thanks to our family and friends
who supported the Wright Bros
in the Autism Speaks walk.

CHAPTER ONE

JENNY Collins stood looking in the storefront window of the Blind Stitch, eyeing the new sign behind the glass.

Beginner's quilting classes starting on Wednesday and Saturday. Everyone welcome.

Okay, it was official—she was in over her head. She was a high-school English teacher, not an expert on quilting. She never should have listened when Allison had told her to jump in with both feet. Unfortunately, Jenny didn't know any other way to do things, and it sometimes got her into trouble.

Yet, her friend had confidence in her. How could she let her down?

Even after Jenny's life had fallen apart, she'd got the manager's job, along with an apartment above the shop, thanks to Allison Casali. The job was hers as long as she wanted to stay in Kerry

Springs, Texas. That was the million-dollar question. How long would she be staying?

The shop door opened, bringing Jenny back to the present, and Millie Roberts poked her head out. In her sixties, Jenny's part-time employee had short, gray hair cut in a flattering style. Petite and slender, Millie was energetic and friendly and, best of all, knowledgeable about quilting.

"We just got a delivery." She smiled. "It's the new fabrics Allison ordered."

Jenny followed her inside the store. "Good, we were getting pretty low on stock."

"Well, that's to be expected since you've sold nearly everything in the store."

They walked past several quilts hanging along the high walls, all custom designs by the shop owner and, most recently, Jenny's boss.

There were stands that displayed colorful bolts of fabrics in every print a quilter could ever want or need. A long cutting table divided the front from the back of the store. A cash register sat on the counter and beside it were several large delivery boxes.

"Oh, boy," Jenny said. "Allison must have bought out the entire wholesale house." She knew the company gave the quilting icon a good deal just to have their textiles associated with the name

Allison Cole Casali. Her loyal followers would buy a lot of their products.

Jenny opened one box and started to remove bolts of colorful fabric. She and Millie were examining the new materials when a soft voice drew Jenny's attention. She turned around to see a small dark-haired girl standing in front of the counter.

The cute child was dressed in a pair of jeans, a pink shirt and white sneakers. Her large blue eyes widened as she gave a tentative smile.

Jenny walked away from the boxes and stopped in front of the girl. "Hello, I'm Jenny Collins."

"I'm Grace Anne Rafferty, but everybody calls me Gracie."

"It's nice to meet you, Gracie Rafferty. This is Millie."

"Hi, Gracie," Millie greeted her, then continued to sort through the boxes.

Jenny turned back to the child. "What can I do for you, Gracie?"

The little girl pointed to the window over her shoulder. "I read the sign. I want you to help me make my quilt."

Jenny glanced at Millie. "Well, Gracie. I don't know." How could she tell the child she was too young? "This class really isn't for children."

"I'm eight years old and I know how to sew. I

even have a quilt started…well, my mother started making it, but she can't help me anymore."

Jenny's heart went out to the child, seeing her sadness. "I wish I could help you, Gracie, but the class is for adults."

The child's shoulders slumped, but her blue eyes widened. "But I hafta finish it 'cause I promised her."

Jenny leaned down to the small child. "Then you and your mother should finish it together. What about if she joins the class?"

The girl shook her head, causing her ponytail to swing back and forth as tears welled in her eyes. "She can't, 'cause she's in heaven."

Evan Rafferty had searched up and down all the aisles of Sayers Hardware, but there was no sign of his daughter anywhere. He hurried outside to his truck, hoping she'd gotten bored and left. Gracie wasn't there either.

He glanced up and down the small town's main street. Where had she gone to? Dear Lord, could someone have taken her? No, not in Kerry Springs. He sent up a silent prayer as he hurried next door to the drug store. Maybe she'd gone in to buy candy. She wasn't there either. He couldn't slow the pounding of his heart, the dread that threatened to overtake him.

He couldn't even take care of his own daughter. Had Megan been right? Maybe he wasn't cut out to be a father.

He rushed past two more storefronts, then stopped suddenly when he saw the patchwork quilts in one of the windows. Gracie had said something about having to finish a quilt.

He pulled open the glass-paneled door and slowed his steps when he heard the sweet voice of his little girl. She'd been the mainstay in his life, the thing that had kept him focused over the past year and a half. The reason he got up every day when some days he wanted to walk away from it all.

Evan passed the rows of shelves stacked high with material until a blond woman came into view, talking to his daughter.

"Gracie Rafferty."

She swung around as her happy look suddenly turned to one of guilt. "Oh, hi, Daddy."

"Don't 'hi, Daddy' me. You know better than to run off." His voice softened, "I couldn't find you."

"I'm sorry," she said as tears welled in her eyes. "You were busy, so I thought I'd come and look at the quilts." She forced a smile that reminded him of her mother.

"None of that excuses you for going off by yourself."

"Mr. Rafferty, I'm Jenny Collins." The blond woman still stood next to his child. "I'm the new manager of the Blind Stitch."

He appraised the storekeeper with her fresh look and easy smile. She was tall and slender, wearing a blue blouse tucked into jeans, accenting a narrow waist and the flare of her hips. When his attention went to her large dark eyes he felt a sudden tightening in his gut.

"I'm sorry you were worried about Gracie," the woman continued. "I didn't know that she didn't have permission to come here."

He reined in his straying thoughts. "What did you think when a child walked in by herself?"

The woman continued to smile, but he could see a flash of anger in her brown-sugar eyes. "I assumed her parent would be coming shortly." She looked down at his daughter. "Gracie, next time you come here make sure you have permission."

The girl nodded as she wiped away a tear. "Okay."

"Good. Now, why don't you go wash your face before your dad takes you home?" The store manager sent him a look as if daring him to challenge her.

An older woman came out from behind the counter. "Hello, Evan."

He felt his cheeks warm as he recognized Millie Roberts. A retired teacher from the school, and a member of the church he'd once attended. He tipped his hat. "Hello, Mrs. Roberts."

"Why don't I take Gracie and show her where to wash up?"

After the two left Jenny turned back to him. "Could I just take a minute of your time, Mr. Rafferty?"

"What's the point? Gracie won't be coming back here."

"Why? Do you have a problem with her taking up quilting? Gracie explained to me that her mother was a quilter and she's been very unhappy since…lately."

Evan didn't want to talk about his private life, especially not with a stranger. "That's not your concern. Besides, Gracie's too young."

Jenny studied this man. She hadn't figured him out yet, only that neither father nor daughter looked happy. From the second she'd seen Gracie standing in front of the counter she'd felt an instant connection to her. Her own childhood hadn't been the happiest, and seeing the girl's sadness nearly broke Jenny's heart.

"Maybe if you take the time to talk to her," she suggested.

"Look, I don't know what makes you an expert,

but I'd appreciate it if you let me handle my daughter."

She nodded. "Your daughter walked in here and involved me in this. I'd like to help. Maybe we can come up with an idea to get her involved in something."

The last thing he needed was another person getting into his business. "No thanks. What I want is to be left alone."

He was grateful when his daughter came out of the restroom. Evan motioned for her. "Come on, Gracie. We need to get back to the ranch."

He headed for the door, Evan didn't know why he was being so rude, both to his daughter and to a woman he didn't even know. It was the woman, that was the problem.

He could understand why Gracie was drawn to her. He glanced back at the pretty blonde. He hated that he felt the same pull. He groaned. He needed to get out more.

"What a jerk," Jenny murmured. "Did you hear him, Millie?" She walked to the store window, not waiting for her coworker's answer. She watched as Mr. Rafferty walked to the curb and helped his daughter into a late-model truck with a logo on the door for Triple R Ranch.

The rancher walked around the cab, giving her

a view of his backside. The tall, loose-limbed cowboy was a killer in a pair of jeans. His thighs were solid and so was his rear end. He had broad shoulders and muscular arms and thick sable hair under his wide-brimmed Stetson.

She could still feel the heat from his smoky blue-eyed stare. Great! For the first time in a long while she felt an attraction to a man, and he definitely wasn't her type. She'd known too many rude and arrogant men like him, including her stepfather. No, she wouldn't waste her time on someone like Evan Rafferty.

She thought back to what the girl had said about her mother being in heaven. Okay, so he'd lost his wife recently. She couldn't help but feel for both of them.

Jenny watched the truck pull away from the curb and Gracie looked in her direction. She waved at her and Jenny's chest tightened with longing. Admittedly the big cowboy had one thing in his favor. The sweetest little girl.

Millie came up beside her. "Don't be too hard on that young man. He's been through a lot." The older woman turned to Jenny, looking sad. "He lost his wife, Megan, a year ago last Thanksgiving."

"What happened?" Jenny found herself asking.

"She had cancer." Millie sighed. "I know she

suffered terribly. Then, not only did Evan have to deal with her death, he's trying to raise a daughter and run his ranch. I don't blame him for being upset when he couldn't find Gracie."

Jenny nodded. She didn't have a child, but she knew what her friend, Allison, had gone through to get her daughter Cherry to walk again after an automobile accident that had nearly taken her life.

She'd probably be as protective if she had a child. She shook away the familiar longing that nagged her and put on a smile.

"Okay, we'd better get back to work," she told Millie. "The beginners' class is scheduled to start in two weeks."

She walked through the store to the new opening in the west wall that led into the building next door. Allison had bought that property when the old tenant had moved out, and the carpenters had finally finished the improvements to expand the shop.

Jenny stood in the doorway and looked at the empty space. They still needed to paint, but new cabinets and shelving lined the far wall. There was plenty of room for class supplies and fabric. And they could bring in the portable sewing machines from storage.

Jenny walked to the area right at the front

window. "What do you think about getting a big round table and some comfortable chairs for this area?"

A bright smile lit up Millie's face. "Women can come here to socialize and quilt."

Jenny shrugged. "A lot of the customers are friends and neighbors. Why not make a place where they can come and work on their projects together, share ideas and tips. We can call it Quilters' Corner. What do you think?"

Millie beamed. "You won't have any trouble filling that table."

Jenny nodded. Good. She had one problem solved, but she was still being nagged by Evan Rafferty. Darn that man for stirring her up. The last thing she needed was a man to disrupt her life right now. She already had enough to deal with.

Yet, she couldn't stop thinking about his daughter. She wanted to do something to help Gracie. An idea suddenly hit her.

"Millie," she began. "If I moved the adult classes to Wednesday and Saturday mornings that would open up time on Saturday afternoons."

Millie hesitated. "What do you have in mind?"

"Maybe a girls' class."

The older woman studied her a moment. "That's a big undertaking because one little girl wants to finish a quilt."

Was that all Gracie wanted? Jenny wondered, thinking back to her own childhood. She had been overshadowed by her stepbrothers and ignored by her stepfather. The worst part was that her mother had let it happen. Maybe that had been Gracie's experience since her mother's death— maybe she felt pushed aside. The big question was, was an eight-year-old too young to join a quilting class?

No.

Jenny looked at Millie. "Do you think some of our regular customers would help out with a mentoring class?

The woman shrugged. "Probably. Is this for any student, or are you talking about one in particular?"

"Maybe, but why can't we help a little girl finish her quilt?"

Millie nodded. "If we're talking about a quilt her mother started, it's not a simple matter. Megan Rafferty was pretty close to an expert quilter. She'd sold several at the local craft fair. But you're right. This could help Gracie, especially since she lives with a houseful of men." A slow smile lit up Millie's face. "All those Rafferty men are a handsome bunch."

Jenny softened thinking about Evan Rafferty,

recalling the raw pain in those eyes. That was her clue to stay clear of the handsome cowboy.

Even without his bad attitude, he still belonged to someone else.

The next afternoon, Jenny headed over to Kerry Springs Elementary School, flyers in hand. She was hoping that the school principal, Lillian Perry, would help promote her class.

When the office door opened she was surprised to see a woman not much older than herself. The attractive brunette smiled as Jenny greeted her and they walked inside.

The principal closed the door. "Thank you for waiting, Ms. Collins."

"Please, call me Jenny."

"And I'm Lily."

After Jenny sat down in a chair, Lily did the same behind her desk. "I hear you've taken over the Blind Stitch."

She nodded. "News travels fast."

"It does in this town. And my mother practically lives at your shop. Beth Staley."

"Oh, of course. She and Millie are friends."

Lily nodded. "So what can I do for you?"

Jenny jumped right in. "I was hoping you could help me promote a children's quilting class." She handed her a flyer. "It's free."

Lily glanced over the paper. "This looks interesting." She eyed Jenny. "Generous, too."

She shrugged. "Call it community service. I'm still not sure how many women I can get to volunteer. Just so you know, I'm asking for your mother's help. It's my plan to pass on the craft to a new generation."

Lily leaned her forearms on the desk. "I'm sure Mother would love it," she told her. "She's been trying to get my daughter, Kasey, interested. Maybe with a class and with other girls her age, she'll want to participate."

They spent the next twenty minutes going over the program; it would not only be good for the young girls to learn a craft, but it would also help them build a relationship with an older generation.

"Blind Stitch will donate fabric and thread, but we'd like to encourage kids to bring in some of their own material. Maybe some blocks cut out of old clothes. Everyone is big on recycling."

"Oh, I love that," Lily said. "Take pride in your family, your heritage." She leaned back in her chair. "I like your enthusiasm, Jenny, and I'll be happy to pass out the flyers to the upper grades." She stood. "Since the bell is about to ring, I need to be out front. I like staying connected to my kids."

"I used to do that," Jenny told her. "Of course, my students were older. High school."

Lily gave her a sideways glance. "You aren't teaching any longer?"

Jenny didn't want to go into details. "I'm taking a semester off for now."

She hated that her attitude about teaching had changed, although never about her students. She would always stand up for the kids; she just didn't always win the fight. "I'll be returning in the fall."

The bell sounded as they walked out the door. In the bright sunlight, chatty students hurried to meet their rides home, but many stopped to greet their principal, Jenny realized she missed that connection she'd once had with her students.

She heard her name called and turned around to see Gracie Rafferty.

"Jenny. Why are you at my school?"

"Hi, Gracie. I came to meet Mrs. Perry."

The girl looked at her principal and smiled. "Hello, Mrs. Perry."

"Hello, Gracie. Jenny came to tell me she's going to have a young girls' quilting class at her shop."

Those big eyes widened. "Really?"

Jenny was glad that made the child happy. "Really. And maybe you can work on your quilt, too," she told her.

The girl seemed excited, but before she could speak again, they heard someone call her name. Jenny glanced around and saw Evan Rafferty standing next to his truck.

The child's smile faded quickly. "I can't. It will make my daddy mad." She turned and ran to the man who had been on Jenny's mind since their first meeting.

"Excuse me, Lily. I need to speak to someone."

Jenny stared over at the truck. She needed to get through to this man, but seeing the stubborn set to Evan Rafferty's jaw, she knew it wasn't going to be easy.

"Mr. Rafferty," she called sweetly. "May I speak with you?"

Evan closed the passenger-side door, then stepped away from the truck and his daughter's hearing. "I'm short on time right now." He gave her the once-over. "Beside, we finished our business the other day."

She ignored him. "Since it's about your daughter, I thought you might spare me a minute."

Evan adjusted the hat on his head and stared into her velvety, brown, dark eyes. He felt a surge of heat. He quickly glanced away.

"Well, you thought wrong. Look, I need to be somewhere right now." *Anywhere away from you.*

He stepped off the curb, climbed into his truck and drove off.

Jenny stood, feeling anger stirring inside. How dare the man… Okay, so she had to figure out another way to help the girl. It wouldn't be the first time she'd fought for a child. She refused to give up on either one of them.

CHAPTER TWO

THE next afternoon, Jenny turned her compact car off the highway, and then along a narrow road until she came to the archway announcing the Triple R Ranch and Rafferty's Vineyard.

This probably wasn't the brightest idea. Yet, she wouldn't stop fighting for kids. She knew what it was like to feel alone, to have no one on your side, especially not your parent. Her own mother had refused to listen to her pleas for help. The teasing, the abuse from stepbrothers who'd been older and should have protected her. They shouldn't have been allowed to pick on an eight-year-old. And no one had done a thing.

Her mother had gotten angry because she'd caused a rift in the family. Family? They were never a family.

Jenny shook away the bad memories. Was that the reason she'd become a crusader for kids? Why she'd wanted to be a teacher? So the young and innocent would have someone to confide in? So they'd know someone was on their side? How many times had she gone the extra mile to help a student succeed? She loved helping kids realize their potential and dreams.

Then it had all fallen apart recently when she'd lost a battle over one of her students. Luis Garcia was excellent college material and she'd worked hard to help him apply for scholarships. Then Luis got into a fight defending another student, and they'd found a knife. Even though the small pocket knife wasn't Luis's, the principal took the word of the other boy and his friends—Luis was expelled immediately.

Jenny begged the principal to at least let him take his mid-term tests, but he'd refused to allow any special consideration.

Jenny knew Luis would never return to school. She was discouraged, too, and took a leave of absence during the spring semester. She needed the time to figure things out, to stop feeling as if she got too involved to be a teacher.

So what did she do now? She went storming into another conflict. She didn't have any business nosing into Gracie's life, but that had never stopped her before. If a child was crying out, she wanted to make sure someone heard. Gracie Rafferty was crying out.

She slowed as she approached the ranch. There

were several head of cattle grazing in the pasture. On the opposite side of the road was a hillside covered in perfect rows of trellises heavy with grapevines. It was breathtaking.

She continued on until she came to a compound with a large barn and a fenced corral. Then a two-story clapboard house appeared, painted a glossy taupe with burgundy shutters and a large welcoming porch. The yard was thick with new spring grass and an array of colorful flowers edged the split-rail fence.

The place looked immaculate.

Jenny pulled up on the gravel parking area and got out. She released several calming breaths as she made her way up the walk. By the time she reached the porch, an elderly gentleman had come out of the house. Big and burly, he had a head of snow-white hair and a broad grin across his face.

"Hello, lass."

She couldn't help but smile back. "Hello. I'm Jenny Collins and I'm looking for Mr. Rafferty."

Still grinning, the man nodded. "And which one of us would you be wantin'? I'm Sean," he said with a slight bow. "Or my sons, Evan and Matthew?"

She could see where Evan got his good looks. Too bad he didn't get his father's charm. "It would be Evan." She glanced around, feeling nervous. "If he isn't busy I'd like to speak with him."

"He isn't here at the moment. Why don't you come in and wait. We'll have some tea."

She hesitated. "I wouldn't want to intrude. If he isn't going to be long, I could wait out here."

Sean motioned for her to step up on the porch. "A pretty lass like yourself would only brighten my day. Please come in."

She couldn't help but smile. "Thank you. I accept your invitation."

Jenny went ahead of Sean and inside the house to the entrance hall. To one side there was a small living room that looked too formal and neat to get much use. Past a staircase with ornate spindles was a dining room with a long table and half a dozen chairs lining either side.

"The Raffertys are an informal bunch. The kitchen is where our hearts are. Around food."

Jenny followed Sean on into the big open room. Miles of cabinets lined the walls, and a solid counter displayed many appliances. There was a natural-stone backsplash that highlighted the area. But it was the wonderful aroma that hit her that made her feel this was truly a home.

"Please, have a seat," Sean told her as he went to the refrigerator. "Would you prefer hot or cold tea?"

"Whatever is easiest for you," she said as she eyed the connected family room with oversized furniture and a television.

"You have a lovely home, Mr. Rafferty."

He set a glass of iced tea in front of her. "First of all, please, call me Sean."

"Only if you call me Jenny."

He nodded and continued. "And secondly, this house belongs to my son Evan and his daughter. My other son Matt and I moved in about a year ago to help out after Evan's wife, Megan, passed away."

She immediately saw his sadness. "I'm sorry for your loss."

He nodded. "Thank you. It's been a rough time for my son and the little one." He looked thoughtful, then finally went on to say, "Anyway, the three of us worked out a partnership." He grinned. "I'm not a rancher, that's Evan's livelihood and it's now Matt's too."

"Is the vineyard yours?"

He shook his head, smiling easily. "It's Evan's, too. I'm just the cook and bottle-washer around here."

Jenny liked this man. Had Evan been this way before his wife's death? "Don't diminish your contribution to the family, Sean. I have a feeling you do more than you're saying."

He leaned against the counter and arched an eyebrow. "I like you, Jenny Collins. So how long have you lived in Kerry Springs?"

"I worked here for a summer two years ago and was here again last summer for a visit, but I returned recently and took over running the Blind Stitch quilt shop."

"I've seen the store. It's across the street from Rory's Bar and Grill. I tend bar there on the weekends."

"Really. I haven't been there."

"It's a nice neighborhood bar. A few friendly games of billiards and darts and a little dancing on weekends. You should stop by sometime." He cocked his head. "But I am curious. What does my son have to do with a quilt shop?"

"It's Gracie. She came into the shop interested in my class."

"Did she now," Sean commented. "Why does that not surprise me? She's been talking about her mother's quilts."

"I'm here to see if there's a way to help her get enrolled."

Sean frowned for the first time. "Good luck with that."

"Daddy," Gracie called. "Can I go to Carrie's house?"

Evan turned the truck off the highway and

glanced in the rearview mirror at his daughter in the backseat. "Not on a school night."

"It's not tonight. It's a party. A sleepover." She hesitated. "All my friends are going to be there and I want to be with them."

Evan wasn't ready to let her go on her own. "If you want, your friends can come to the house and play."

Evan looked at his brother, Matt, in the passenger seat. Usually Matt had never been shy about speaking his mind. Yet, since his return from overseas, he'd pretty much kept to himself, working the cattle operation and taking up residence in the foreman's house.

His dad, on the other hand, had voiced his opinion many times about him isolating Gracie.

"Daddy," Gracie called again. "She's having a sleepover. And her older sister is going to put makeup on us and paint our toes and fingernails with any color we want."

He tensed. She was too young for all that stuff. "I'll think about it."

Matt didn't stay quiet this time. "It wouldn't hurt to let her go. Give her that girl experience."

Evan kept his voice low and controlled. "I don't think Gracie will be deprived if she doesn't get her toes painted."

"How do you know that? You're not a little girl. We got to do boy things when we were growing up."

They'd had a rough childhood, especially after their mother had taken off, leaving her husband and sons. They'd been left unsupervised more than they should have been. It might not have been the typical home life, but they'd always got plenty of love from their dad.

"And look how much trouble we got into," Evan told his brother.

A smile kicked at the corners of Matt's mouth. "We survived, Evan. Kids need to learn how to deal with things."

"Gracie has had to deal with enough already. So can we let it go for now?"

"Why? So *you* don't have to deal with it? Gracie doesn't have a problem. It's you, bro. You're the one who hasn't moved on."

Evan turned his attention toward the house and saw a strange car parked out front. He parked in his usual spot at the back and they walked into the house through the kitchen door. He heard laughter, then his breath caught when he saw Jenny Collins sitting on the bar stool talking with his father.

She was dressed in a pair of dark jeans with black boots and a red blouse under a short black jacket. Her blond hair hung past her shoulders in thick waves. He was suddenly irritated at the feelings she stirred up, feelings he'd thought were long gone.

"Man, oh, man," Matt murmured as he removed his cowboy hat and placed it on the hook. "I think I've died and gone to heaven."

His father finally noticed them. "Well, you're home."

Gracie came in behind them. "Jenny," she cried and went to her. "You came to my house."

"Yes, I did." Jenny glanced at Evan. "I hope that's not a problem."

Not happy with the surprise, Evan hung up his hat, then crossed the family room. "Gracie, go put your books away and change into your play clothes."

She started to argue, but then did as her father asked. "Don't go away, Jenny," she called. "I'll be right back. I want to show you something."

Jenny sent a challenge to Evan. "I promise I'll be here when you get back."

Everyone watched as Gracie walked out. But before Evan could speak, his father began, "Jenny Collins, this is my other son, Matt."

Jenny smiled at a younger version of Evan, but one with an easy smile and dark bedroom eyes. And he knew how to use them.

"Well, hello, Jenny," he said and took her hand.

"You must be new in town, or my eyesight is going if I passed you by without as much as a hello."

She laughed. "It's nice to meet you, too, Matt. And yes, I recently took over the quilt shop in town, that's why I'm here. I need to convince your brother that his daughter would be perfect for our class. I know Gracie is interested in joining us."

"That sounds like a great idea," Matt said.

Evan jumped in. "It's not a good idea, because I don't have time to bring her in."

Jenny wasn't giving up. "Surely we can work out something, Mr. Rafferty. She's told me how much she wants to finish her quilt."

Evan frowned. "I haven't seen any quilt."

Jenny was afraid she'd given away a secret. "Maybe you should ask your daughter about it."

"I plan to."

Jenny wasn't sure what to do now. The man had dismissed her, but she couldn't leave without seeing Gracie.

Sean stepped in. "I know Gracie will want to show you her project. And Jenny, we would like you to stay for supper."

Jenny hesitated, but Sean smiled at her.

"It's my famous beef stew," he told her. She glanced at Evan. His stoic look was meant to drive her away. She refused to let it.

"Oh, my, how can I turn that down? Thank you.

I accept." She glanced around, trying to avoid looking at Evan Rafferty. "Is there anything I can do to help?"

Sean waved his hand. "Oh, no, you're a guest."

There was a sound of footsteps on the stairs, then Gracie came running into the room a little breathless. "Good. You're still here."

She stroked the child's hair. "I told you I wouldn't leave."

"And she's staying for supper," her grandfather told her. "Now, go and show Jenny where to wash up."

Gracie's eyes lit up. "You want to see my room?"

"Of course, I'd love to." Jenny held out her hand and Gracie took it. Together they walked out.

Angry about being blindsided, Evan turned to his father. "What are you doing?"

"It's called being neighborly. Something you seem to have forgotten as of late. I never thought I'd see the day when one of my sons would be rude to a guest in his home. It's time you climbed out of the cave you've buried yourself in. It might be what you want, but your daughter needs more."

Matt elbowed him. "Yeah, bro. And man, she's one pretty lady." He looked at his dad. "If you hadn't invited her, I would have."

Sean raised a hand. "Simmer down, Matt. Jenny's interest is in Gracie. Even she can see the child needs more. And look here, son, help came knocking on the door."

Evan didn't like everyone invading his life. He just wanted to be left alone.

His father grew serious as he looked at him. "It wouldn't hurt for the little one to have some female companionship. So, son, don't go looking at this gift as if it's a curse."

Jenny glanced around the small yellow-and-lavender bedroom as Gracie showed off the row of her favorite dolls on a shelf along the wall. The hardwood floors were covered with a natural-colored area rug. There was a white twin bed that was covered with a patchwork quilt.

"My mom made me this quilt for my birthday when I was six."

Jenny examined the detail on the Country Hearts pattern. The colorful heart appliqués sat inside each of the many six-inch blocks. The sashing was a wide strip of a lavender print. It was well done.

"This is so pretty." Jenny looked at Gracie. "Your mother did beautiful work."

The girl smiled. "She made a lot more. You want to see?"

"Sure."

Gracie motioned for her to follow. They went

down the hall into another bedroom. The second
Jenny stepped inside she knew she shouldn't be
here. Yet, she couldn't leave what was obviously
the master bedroom. The beautiful large four-
poster bed was covered in a solid navy comforter.

Gracie went to a cedar chest at the end of the
bed. "They're in there. Daddy put them all away
after Mommy…died."

Jenny felt as if she was intruding. "Maybe we
should leave them for another time." She glanced
across the room at the dresser and saw the many
framed family pictures. She recognized a young-
er-looking Evan standing next to a dark-haired
woman who was holding a toddler, Gracie. And
he was smiling. She doubted he did much of that
lately.

She quickly turned away from the loving scene.
"I don't want us to get into trouble."

The child struggled to lift the lid. "But my quilt
is in here." The child looked panicked. "It's mine."

Jenny had no choice but to help her. She opened
the heavy lid and discovered the treasure inside.
There were several colorful quilts folded neatly.
The top one was an amazing Bow Tie-patterned
quilt in shades of blues and burgundy. The back-
ground was cream-colored with intertwined
blocks of printed fabric.

Megan Rafferty definitely wasn't an amateur.

Gracie continued to dig underneath. "See, there it is."

Jenny lifted out the plastic-covered blanket. She removed the covering and spread it out on the bed. The Wedding Ring design was only partly finished, but there were several rings already sewn together, and several other stacks were in the bag.

"Mommy and I picked out all the colors, but she got too sick to sew anymore." A sad Gracie looked at Jenny. "She had to stay in bed all the time."

Jenny couldn't resist and sat down, pulled the small girl onto her lap and hugged her close. No child should have to go through that kind of loss.

Gracie laid her head against Jenny's shoulder. "I didn't get to see her very much 'cause she was always sleeping."

She had no doubt Megan Rafferty fought valiantly to keep going for her child.

"Oh, honey, it wasn't because your mom didn't want you around her. She was trying to fight to get better. Just look how she worked to make you this quilt."

The girl raised her head, revealing tears. "That's what she told me when I went to say goodbye to her. She said that I have to finish it for her. I promised her. I hafta do it."

Evan stood in the hall outside his bedroom. It

had always been Meg's domain. She'd decorated the room, trying to make it perfect. It was—to an outsider. Yet this room had never been his sanctuary, even less so now—with the guilt he felt that he'd let his wife down. Now he was letting Gracie down.

Watching her, he felt another kind of pain. Jenny Collins was holding his daughter, stroking her hair, whispering words to soothe her sadness. Gracie couldn't come to him, but she turned to a stranger.

When Jenny looked up, discovering him, it was he who suddenly felt like the intruder. Her dark-eyed gaze locked with his. He couldn't read her thoughts. Did she think he was a bad father? What did he care what she thought? She was the one intruding on his life.

Jenny saw Evan Rafferty in the hall. She held her breath, hoping that he wouldn't interrupt them. His daughter desperately needed to share some of her pain. She needed to let out her feelings without worrying about anyone else.

Jenny brushed tears from the child's face. "What else did your mother tell you?"

Gracie looked thoughtful. "She asked me to be a good girl."

"And you are," Jenny confirmed. "What else?"

"To help Daddy 'cause he'll be all alone." Those pretty sapphire eyes locked on hers. Her daddy's eyes. "I don't know how."

Jenny had to swallow hard to move the lump from her throat. "Oh, sweetie. It will take time. Maybe if you both share all the good times together. Tell stories about your mom so you'll always remember her."

Gracie smiled. "Maybe I can tell him how much fun it was sewing the quilt with Mommy. Maybe he'll let me go to your class."

Jenny's heart tightened painfully. "Maybe. But if he doesn't agree right now, maybe he will later. You can wait," she said positively. "Your mommy will understand."

Gracie hugged her. "I'm glad you came to see me, Jenny. Will you be my friend?"

Jenny swallowed back tears and hugged the child to her heart. "Oh, of course, Gracie." She glanced over to find Evan was still there. Her chest tightened, seeing that his child's words had affected him, too.

That wasn't all she felt. Their gazes connected as she suddenly became aware of the man's powerful presence. Yet, underneath, she could sense sadness, a loneliness that pulled at her. She felt the longing, too. A rush of heat went through her and she couldn't look away.

That was when she realized that *all* the Raffertys were getting to her.

CHAPTER THREE

An hour later, Evan sat at the dining-room table drinking his wine. The laughter was getting to him, but he found it hard to join in. He watched Gracie with Jenny, recalling what had taken place upstairs in the bedroom.

His daughter's sadness ran deep, and he couldn't seem to help her. Yet, this woman had an easy, comforting way with the child. He envied that.

He turned to his brother. Matt seemed infatuated with her, too. That was a good thing, wasn't it? It seemed his brother was returning to that happy and carefree guy he remembered.

His attention returned to Ms. Collins. She was attractive with those big brown eyes and silky wheat-colored hair. He felt a stirring of interest, but told himself it was because he hadn't been with anyone in a long time. Even months before Meg died, they hadn't shared any intimacy. Not that they had shared much before that, either. So it wasn't exactly headline news that the sight of a pretty woman would push his buttons.

He took another drink of the zinfandel. The fruity taste—strawberry and raspberry—had just enough sweetness with a hint of oak. Pride struck him, knowing he'd helped produce the grapes for this vintage.

His father leaned toward him. "It's so natural between them," he said, nodding toward the two females. "It does my heart good to watch them."

Evan knew that Gracie missed her mother. He'd hated hearing her crying at night, hated even more that he didn't know how to comfort her. Meg had been the loving, nurturing one. She and Gracie had had the close bond he'd never managed with his daughter.

He studied Jenny. She had that same easy way with kids, with the rest of the family, too. He wasn't going to let himself get taken in by the pretty woman. He didn't need the distraction, and too many people could get hurt if things didn't work out. His main concern now was his daughter.

"Gracie, I think it's time for you to get bathed and ready for bed."

She started to argue, then looked at Jenny. "Will you come and say goodnight?"

Jenny glanced at Evan. "Sure. I'll help clean up here and be right up."

"Okay." The child stood and scurried out of the room.

Jenny looked at Evan's father. "Dinner was delicious, Sean."

"Then have another glass of wine, and savor it a little longer," he insisted.

She shook her head. "Although it was wonderful, I have to drive back into town. Now, no argument, I am going to help you with the dishes." She stood, stacked some plates and carried them into the kitchen.

Sean turned to Evan. "You're coming, too. Because whether you believe it or not, you need to speak to Jenny about Gracie. And listen to her, son." Sean headed out, and Evan followed. He hated that his father was right. Hated that he couldn't seem to make Gracie happy.

In the kitchen Matt was already beside Jenny when they got there, but his father stepped in. "Lass, you get away from the sink. It's Matt's turn to clean up. Besides, most everything goes into the dishwasher." He glanced at his eldest son. "Evan, why don't you show Jenny around the vineyard?"

That was subtle.

Jenny looked stunned. "Oh, there's no need, Sean. I'll go up and see Gracie, then I should get back to town."

"There's plenty of daylight left. And I'll keep

my granddaughter occupied until you return." He leaned toward her. "You wanted to talk to Evan, now's your chance." He motioned to the door and practically pushed them both outside.

Jenny could tell that Evan didn't like the idea of them being thrown together any more than she did. That bothered her. Except for her stepbrothers, she wasn't used to people not liking her. She worked hard to make friends.

"You don't have to do this, Mr. Rafferty."

"It's Evan." He tugged on his hat as he walked her toward a golf cart. "Jenny."

She sat in the passenger seat as he walked around and climbed in. He drove off toward the hillside. "I usually walk, but this will be faster."

"And you can get rid of me quicker."

He shook his head, but didn't say a word as they rode past the barn and took a trail up the bumpy hillside for about a half mile. The spring evening was nice. Quiet. Serene. Peaceful.

The cart stopped at the edge of the rise, he got out and she did the same, but had to hurry to keep up. The sun was just going down as they walked toward the rows of vines.

"The tour isn't necessary, Evan. I only came out here to ask you a question about Gracie. I never planned to get invited to supper or involved in your life, your family."

When he stopped suddenly, she nearly ran into him. He reached out and caught her, his touch burning through her skin; his grip tightened on her arms, but his strength didn't hurt. Then their eyes locked and suddenly she couldn't breathe. When she managed to suck in some air, she inhaled his scent of soap and sun-dried cotton. His gaze shifted to her mouth, then suddenly he blinked and released her.

With a curse, he turned away and looked out at the vineyard. Removing his hat, he raked his fingers through his hair as if gathering his thoughts.

He glanced back at her. "Look, I'm not social like the rest of my family. I prefer to be left alone." His gaze met hers. "I have no excuse for my behavior the other day in the shop except I was worried when Gracie came up missing."

Jenny could see the anguish on his face. "That's understandable," she agreed. "She shouldn't have run off without telling you."

"It seems she wants to spend less and less time with me."

"She's growing up." Jenny saw the sadness in his eyes. "But there's no mistaking that your little girl adores you."

He straightened at her words. "I wouldn't say that. We're both having trouble finding our way around each other. Gracie and her mother were close."

"It's got to be hard for both of you."

"I've been doing okay."

They began walking through a row of vines.

"You're lucky to have Sean and Matt helping out," she said, wondering what it would be like to have family on your side.

Evan sent her a look. What did she think about Matt? He'd always been the more outgoing brother, especially when it came to the ladies. Was Jenny attracted to him? He stopped his thoughts. Why the hell did he care? He didn't want a relationship. So far he'd been lousy at them.

They made their way to the hilltop and looked down the other side. He felt an ache in his chest as he saw the clearing where a large framed structure stood. Deserted. Incomplete. All construction had stopped two years ago, along with his future dreams.

Before he could steer Jenny back to the cart, she asked, "What's that?"

"It was to be the winery."

"Oh, you're expanding?"

"Not any more," he told her, then turned away.

She nodded, but didn't stop. "How long have you had the vineyard?"

The long-time dream replayed in his mind. He

continued to stare out at the vines. "The land belonged to my wife's family, the Kerchers. As you know, a lot of Germans settled in this area. My in-laws planted the vines originally, then about six years ago when her parents passed away, Megan inherited the place and we expanded the acreage."

"So you became an instant winemaker," Jenny said.

"Actually Meg was already one when we met." He'd give her the minimal information. "She'd gotten her degree at Cal Poly in California. I'm just your average, everyday cowboy."

She studied him a moment. "I doubt, Evan Rafferty, that you do anything just average. My bet is you know every grape on this land."

He ignored the funny sensation caused by her compliment and started back through another row of vines. "I thought you wanted to talk about Gracie."

She nodded. "Of course. I want your daughter to come to my class."

When he started to speak, she raised a hand. "I know it's difficult for you to bring her into town every week. What if we find an alternative to help you out?" She hesitated. "She wants to finish the quilt her mother started for her."

He'd hoped that he could put this off a while longer. "I don't think that's a good idea."

"Is it not a good idea for her, or for you?"

He glared at her. "Doesn't make any difference."

Trying to remain calm, Jenny glanced around at the vines heavy with grapes. She'd dealt with obstinate parents before. "It does to Gracie. She's going through a rough time and this focus on the quilt is how she's dealing with her loss."

Evan stopped. His sapphire-blue gaze locked on hers, causing her breath to grow labored. "And how is this class supposed to do this?" he asked.

The man was driving her crazy. "Remember, for the past year and a half your daughter has lived in a household of only men. It's important for little girls to have other females to talk to," she said, seeing by his blank look that she wasn't getting through to him.

"Why are you such an expert?"

"Because your daughter picked me. Also, I had three stepbrothers who made my life miserable and a mother who was too busy for me." Darn, she hadn't meant to tell him that.

He frowned at her, but she wouldn't let him ask any questions.

"Look, I don't know you, Evan, but I know your daughter is reaching out. Don't dismiss that."

"That's right, you don't know me, or what my life's been like trying to run this place and raise a child."

"I apologize if I spoke out of turn." She released a breath, hating that she still thought about her own rotten childhood, and especially about her youngest stepbrother, Todd. "We should go back. Gracie's probably wondering where I am."

She'd started toward the golf cart when Evan reached for her.

"Dammit, Jenny, I'm not the bastard you think I am."

She shook her head. "I never said that." She closed her eyes momentarily. "I never should have come here." Once again she was getting involved in something that was none of her business.

"Too late now," he murmured as they sat in the cart.

She was thankful that Evan didn't comment anymore, but drove her back to the house. She didn't need to get involved with this man or his family. She'd been there before. Cared about a man who couldn't get past his first love. Not that she was looking for a relationship with Evan. Her hope was to help Gracie find closure.

They walked through the back door to find Sean and Matt still in the kitchen.

"Well, that didn't take much time."

"I need to get back to town." She smiled at Sean. "Thank you so much for supper, it was wonderful."

Evan's father grinned. "Any time, lass." He pulled her into a big bear hug. She couldn't help but close her eyes and revel in the comfort of those big arms, then reluctantly step away, turning to his younger son.

"It was nice to meet you, too, Matt."

"It was my pleasure." He hugged her too. "Hey, don't let this guy run you off." He nodded toward Evan. "I'll protect you from him."

Evan wanted to slug his brother. Why did everyone think he was such a grouch? He caught his reflection in the mirror over the family-room mantel and saw his grim look. Damn.

Jenny started out of the room. "I'll go and say goodnight to Gracie."

Evan watched her leave, wanting to follow her, but knowing Gracie probably wouldn't appreciate the intrusion.

His father came up next to him. "Don't chase her off, son. At the very least Jenny Collins is willing to help with Gracie."

Evan glared. He wasn't ready for this. "Maybe I don't want her help."

Matt moved closer. "Oh, boy, I'd take her help in a second."

"You stay away from her. She's not your type."

Matt exchanged a look with his father before he turned to Evan. "She's pretty. So she's my type."

"She's befriended Gracie, and I think that should come first, before you finding your girl of the month."

From Matt's earliest years, he'd had a well-known reputation with the ladies around town. He'd probably dated just about every girl in the county. Now, his eyes lit up. "Do I hear a little jealousy in your voice?" He slapped Evan on the shoulder. "Welcome back, bro."

Jenny went upstairs to Gracie's room. She wanted to make this quick, before she ran into Evan again.

She peeked in the door and smiled at the little girl sitting in bed, looking at a book. "Hey, sweetie."

"Jenny." Gracie motioned for her to come in. "Sit with me."

She walked toward the bed and sat down. "For a little while."

Gracie looked sad. "Did Daddy get mad at you 'cause you want to help with Mommy's quilts?"

Jenny quickly shook her head. It didn't matter if he was. "No." She brushed back the girl's bangs. "Your dad and I just talked awhile. How do feel when you look at your mother's things?"

"A little sad, but mostly happy." The girl glanced away. "I wish… I wish I could talk to her again."

"I know, honey. That part is hard. But you can

still talk to her." Jenny glanced up at the ceiling. "She's up there watching over you."

"That's what Papa Sean says."

Jenny nodded. "She might not be able to answer you, but she's listening. And if it makes you feel good to talk to her, then you should."

This time Gracie nodded and looked upward. "Mom? Mom, I want to sew your quilt, but Daddy doesn't want me to. He says I'm too little. I think he's sad 'cause you went away."

Jenny forced a smile. "Now, tell her something that makes you happy."

"I got an A on my spelling test." The girl looked thoughtful. "And Carrie asked me to come to her house for a sleepover, but Daddy won't let me go. He thinks I'm still a baby." Gracie looked at Jenny. "Will you talk to him about that, too?"

Jenny was now catching on to this child's plan. "Oh, Gracie, that's between you and your dad."

"But you asked him to let me come to your class."

"And I'm still working on that."

"But I hafta go to the sleepover. If I don't everybody will call me a baby." Tears flooded her eyes. "And I won't have any friends."

"Gracie, that's not true. Real friends stick by you." How could she convince a little girl to believe that when life had already thrown her the hardest knock of all? She glanced up and saw Evan walk into the room.

He must have heard Gracie crying. "What's wrong?"

Gracie shook her head and buried her face against Jenny's blouse. "Nothing."

"It isn't 'nothing' when it makes you cry." He sent a look toward Jenny. "Tell me and maybe I can fix it."

The girl sat up straight, wiped her tears and announced, "I want to go to Carrie's sleepover."

Evan knew he'd walked into that one. "Gracie, you're too young."

"All the other girls get to go, and she's my best friend."

Jenny glared at him. "Best friends are important. Didn't you have a best friend?"

He ignored her. "You can have your friends over here."

"Really? You mean it?"

He nodded, relieved that his daughter was so receptive to the idea. "Sure."

"A sleepover!" Gracie was so excited. "I get to have a sleepover."

Evan shifted uncomfortably. He didn't remember agreeing to that. "Well, huh, that might not be a good idea, since there aren't any women living here. Some of the mothers might not like that."

Gracie looked thoughtful. "What about Jenny? She's a girl."

Jenny's eyes widened. "I'm not sure that's what your dad wants, Gracie."

Evan decided to play her game. "Wait. That might work," he told Jenny. "You could organize whatever kids do. I bet you could recruit a lot of girls for your class. Maybe you could even work on Gracie's quilt."

"Oh, Daddy, no." Gracie shook her head. "That's not what girls do at sleepovers. We do things like put on makeup and do our hair, paint our toenails. We get to stay up all night and watch videos."

"Sounds like fun." He looked at Jenny. "But you still have to be supervised by an adult woman."

Evan knew he was crazy for involving this woman in his life, his daughter's life, but he was desperate. Gracie was growing up and she needed things he didn't know how to give her.

"I guess it's up to Jenny."

She studied him, then murmured, "You think you're pretty smart, don't you, Rafferty?" Then she turned a sweet smile toward Gracie. "I think your daddy and I need to discuss this...alone." She leaned down and kissed Gracie's cheek and whispered. "You get some sleep."

"Okay. Night, Jenny. Night, Daddy." After a quick kiss from her father, the child burrowed under the blanket and closed her eyes. If he didn't know better, he'd think his daughter had set him up.

"Good night, Gracie." He closed the bedroom door and walked down the steps behind Jenny. Without a word, she grabbed her purse off the table at the door and walked out.

He hurried after her. "Jenny. Wait."

She stopped on the walkway. Night had fallen, and the only illumination was from the porch light. "What do you want now, Rafferty?"

"Nothing. Nothing at all." He studied her. "Why are you angry? You came out here and got involved in this. I didn't ask you to come. So don't get all bent out of shape when my daughter starts clinging to you."

She folded her arms across her chest. "Maybe that should give you a clue."

"About what?"

"That you don't know much about women."

He stiffened. "What's that supposed to mean?"

"You don't want to hear what I have to say."

He moved closer. "Give it to me straight. I can handle it."

"You're prejudiced, Rafferty. If Gracie was a boy, I'd bet he'd be able to go to sleepovers."

He opened his mouth to disagree, but ended up closing it. "It's different with a boy."

She groaned. "I've heard that so many times I could scream. Then tell me this, if you had a son, would you bring him into town to play Little League games? This quilting class is your daughter's baseball game. Give this time to her, and you won't regret it."

He felt like a jerk. She was right. "Okay, Gracie will be there next Saturday."

She smiled at him and his belly tightened. "Don't worry, Rafferty. I'll make it as painless as possible."

He knew that was a lie. He was already hurting for her, but he'd find a way to put a stop to that. The only female he wanted a relationship with was his daughter. He needed to make sure a certain pretty blonde didn't cause any more complications in his life.

CHAPTER FOUR

THE following Saturday afternoon, Jenny wished she could rethink her idea of this class. Several girls between the ages of eight and twelve were running around, chattering away with the occasional high-pitched squeal. When she suggested they find their seats, they ignored her. Thank goodness for the mothers and her helpers.

Her friend, the shop's owner Allison, walked in. The petite auburn-haired mother of three smiled as she glanced around the new classroom area. "Oh, Jenny, you did a wonderful job with this space."

"Thanks. Millie helped a lot, too."

They both eyed the new shelves along the wall. Every nook had the name of a student, with room for their projects. "I thought if they kept their quilts here they would have less chance of getting lost or dirty."

They walked toward the large round table at the window and Jenny announced, "The Quilters' Corner."

With a smile, Allison nodded. "Has anyone claimed time here yet?"

Jenny nodded. "A few of Millie's friends came in yesterday. They had coffee and went through a few pattern books. We'll see what happens."

"It might take time and the classes are a start. Not only kids are here, but their mothers."

"And I'd better get things started."

Jenny went to the front and suddenly the room grew quiet. With a smile, she said, "Hello, girls. Ladies."

"Hello, Miss Jenny," they answered in unison.

"Are you ready to start your projects?"

Again they answered in unison, with a "Yes." A pang of regret hit her as she thought about her class back in San Antonio, and the students she'd had to leave.

"Okay, then." She began to walk between the rows of tables. "I see most of you have brought in your fabric. For those of you who haven't, there are several bolts on the shelves, along with any other supplies you'll need." She smiled. "So let's get started. We might not get to do any sewing today, but we can cut out blocks of fabric."

As the teams began their first task, Jenny stopped and talked to each girl along with her mother. She was happy to see Principal Perry's daughter, Kasey, there with her grandmother, loyal customer, Beth Staley.

There were ten twosomes. Even Allison's daughter, eight-year-old Cherry, was here to work on her family quilt. That was good, since Jenny hoped to use her friend's expertise to help with the class.

The one disappointment was that she didn't see Gracie Rafferty. Evan had gone back on his word.

"Gracie didn't show?" Allison asked as she stood back from Cherry, who was busy using a cutter on her fabric.

Jenny shook her head. "I did everything I could to get her here. I even offered to drive her in."

Her friend smiled. "It's one of the things that's so endearing about you, Jenny Collins. You want to help everyone, but there are some out there who don't want it."

"I know, but Gracie was so eager to finish her mother's quilt."

"And she will…someday."

No sooner did the words come out than Gracie Rafferty came rushing through the door. She was out of breath when she asked Jenny, "Am I too late?"

"No, you're in time," Jenny assured her and pointed to an empty space she'd saved. "You can sit here."

Gracie beamed as she took her place in front of the portable sewing machine and next to Cherry. Jenny had planned it that way, knowing Gracie would need Allison's help with the complicated pattern.

Evan Rafferty appeared in the doorway. Jenny hated the way she reacted to the man dressed in worn jeans, a navy Henley T-shirt and dusty boots.

She'd been born and raised in Texas, but somehow this man gave a whole new meaning to the word *cowboy*. It seemed many of the other women in the room were sizing him up, too.

With hat in hand, Evan walked toward her carrying a large shopping bag. "She'll need this." He gave it to Jenny and she looked inside to find the quilt from the cedar chest.

"Thank you, Evan, for letting Gracie join the class."

He nodded and they walked back toward the doorway and out of earshot. "I didn't go back on my word, Jenny. I hope you don't either."

Jenny knew she'd never do that to sweet little Gracie. "I don't go back on my word, either, Rafferty. In your daughter's case, I definitely think the class will help her. It's important to her that she finishes this. What better place than with other girls her age? Where she isn't outnumbered by men."

They both glanced toward Gracie's workspace. Millie was helping the girl lay out her fabric and the Double Wedding Ring cutting template. "Look at her, Evan. You have a determined child."

Evan didn't like feeling helpless. The day he'd found out about Meg's cancer, he'd known he couldn't fix it. He couldn't save her. Worst of all, he couldn't keep his daughter from losing her mother. It was a natural instinct to protect his child. It seemed he'd been doing it all wrong.

"She's a lot like her mother." There hadn't been many things that Meg had left unfinished. No doubt Gracie had decided to pick up where she'd left off.

He quickly drew his attention away from Gracie and looked at Jenny. The woman looked like a breath of fresh air and bright sunshine. Her hair was pulled up in a ponytail and she wore a yellow knit top with a long print skirt that seemed to flow against her generous curves.

She'd kept him distracted all week. He didn't like that much.

"All Gracie has talked about all week is you and the sleepover." His gaze locked on hers. "If you don't have the time, let me know now."

Jenny looked surprised at his directness. "The question is, Rafferty, are you ready for a half dozen little girls and me?"

No way was he ready for her. "Not sure I can handle it, but I'll try." He glanced away. "When will the class be finished?"

Jenny blinked. "In two hours." She glanced at the clock. "Three o'clock. Of course, the game could go extra innings."

He caught the baseball analogy and fought a smile as the high-pitched chatter of little girls serenaded them. "I don't think you're ready for extra innings, teacher. I'll be back at three." He said goodbye to his daughter and walked out.

She watched Evan leave, as did the other adult women in the room. The man wasn't even aware of his sex appeal.

Allison appeared beside her. "Okay, what's going on?"

Caught, Jenny glanced away. "Nothing. Evan only wanted to know what time class ended."

Her friend crossed her arms. "And I'm talking about the intense heat between you two."

Jenny shook her head. "No heat. I barely know the man. Besides, I'm not falling for another cowboy." Two summers ago she'd nearly given up everything for the Casalis' ranch foreman.

"Brian wasn't the man for you." Allison's green eyes sparkled. "But someone like Evan Rafferty I can see you with. Good-looking. Sexy. He has a cute little girl, and most importantly he seems very interested, too."

Jenny knew that wasn't true. "What are you doing looking at another man?"

"Since I'm married to a hot Italian, I recognize attraction when I see it. And you two were throwing off sparks."

Jenny lowered her voice. "Nothing is going to happen between Rafferty and me. He's recently widowed." She wasn't sure he was ready. "And besides, I'm going back to San Antonio soon."

Allison watched her. "I was hoping you'd think about staying here permanently," she said, then quickly added, "And what better way than to find a great guy?"

A few years ago, Allison had been lucky to find Alex Casali. He'd come into her life when she was at her lowest point, with an injured daughter and an ex-husband who had taken nearly everything from her. Alex had helped her with Cherry's therapy and got the little girl walking again.

It was a fairy-tale ending when the handsome, wealthy rancher had fallen in love with the single mother. Now married, they'd added a set of eighteen-month-old twins, Will and Rose, to complete the perfect package.

At thirty-two, Jenny wanted to find the same thing, but she realized it might never happen. The one thing she wasn't about to settle for was less, as her mother had.

"What makes you say Evan Rafferty is a great guy?" she asked.

Allison glanced away, then back at her. "When Megan died, I remember hearing what a great couple they were. Alex had met Evan and his wife at a Cattleman's Association meeting. He said Megan talked about building their winery and getting out of the cattle business."

Jenny remembered seeing the herd grazing in the pasture. "Can't he do both?"

"I believe Evan is doing whatever he can to hang on to it all. His wife's long illness cost a lot financially."

Jenny thought about the beautiful Triple R. No doubt Evan and his wife had put a lot of work into it. She also remembered the half-finished winery. Like the unfinished quilt. It was as if Evan just stopped dreaming altogether.

Surprisingly, three o'clock came fast. Although tired, Jenny was also invigorated by the kids' enthusiasm. Luckily she had experts there to answer the hard questions, but she was concerned about Gracie's ambitious project. A Wedding-Ring quilt wasn't a design for an eight year old. It was even pushing her own skills to the limits.

As the students cleared their areas, Jenny helped Gracie, and Allison did the same with her daughter. The two girls knew each other from school, but they were in different classrooms. Today they had become fast friends.

Cherry turned to her mother. "Mommy, can Gracie go riding with us tomorrow?"

Allison hesitated and then smiled at her daughter. "Of course, as long as it's okay with her father."

Gracie was hesitant with her response. "My daddy probably won't let me 'cause I can't go anywhere by myself."

"Why don't we ask him?" Jenny said, hoping the man would give his daughter some family time.

"Ask me what?"

They all turned as Evan arrived to pick up his daughter.

"Daddy." Gracie took his hand and pulled him to the group. "This is Cherry and we're friends."

He nodded at the child with the strawberry-blond curls. "Hello, Cherry."

The young girl smiled. "Hello, Mr. Rafferty."

Evan looked at Jenny. "How'd it go?"

"Fine. Gracie got a lot started today." She glanced at her friend, hoping that Evan didn't sense her concern about Gracie's complicated project. "Thanks to Allison. Allison, this is Evan Rafferty. Evan, Allison Casali."

He nodded. "It's nice to meet you, Mrs. Casali. I've spoken with your husband a few times."

Her friend shook his hand. "Please, call me Allison. You must have done most of the talking, because Alex is a man of few words."

Evan gave a hint of a smile. "He doesn't need to say much."

At a nudge from Cherry, Gracie spoke up. "Daddy, Cherry asked me to come to her house and go riding."

Jenny watched as Evan started to shake his head. "I don't think that's possible right now. I need to get back to the ranch."

Seeing the girls' disappointment, Allison said, "Look, girls, go put away your things in your cubbyholes. Make sure your names are on them." After they'd left, she turned to Evan. "We usually go riding on Sunday afternoons. It started as Cherry's therapy reward. Since the automobile accident three years ago, she's worked hard to walk again. She'd really like it if Gracie came along."

Jenny stood back as Allison charmed the man. "Does Gracie ride?" her friend asked.

"Yes, although it's been awhile but—"

"Of course, you're invited, too. Alex is going along." She grew serious. "I refuse to let my husband work on Sunday. It's family time." She glanced at Jenny. "And, of course, Jenny will be there. She's been working too much overtime." She looked back at Evan. "I can't tell you how special it would make the day for Cherry."

Evan hesitated, then said, "I'll have to see."

Allison scribbled down a phone number and handed it to him. "We plan to ride out to Lucky Creek for a picnic. If you decide to come, we leave about eleven."

Evan had been caught off guard by Allison Casali's invitation. He looked at Jenny. He didn't want to spend more time with her. She'd already managed to weave herself into his life.

Just then the girls came back, both looking at him for his answer. It was Allison Casali who helped him out. "If Mr. Rafferty can't bring Gracie out tomorrow to ride, we'll do it another time."

Gracie looked up at him with a sparkle in her eyes that he hadn't seen in a long time. He had trouble taking a breath. Did it take so little to make her happy?

"Maybe we can make time tomorrow," he said.

"Really?"

"Yes, really," he promised.

He leaned down to take her sweet hug. Her arms felt so good. "Thank you, Daddy," she whispered.

"You're welcome, Gracie." He released her and she went off with her new friend.

He stood and caught Jenny watching him. He could see that she approved of what he'd done.

"Seems my daughter's social life has picked up since you've come to town." He looked into her eyes. Suddenly he was pulled into those dark depths. "Don't expect mine to do the same."

"Look out, Rafferty, you've already started by accepting the Casalis' invitation. Just try to enjoy yourself."

He wasn't sure he remembered how to enjoy himself, but he suddenly realized he was looking forward to tomorrow.

The next day was sunny when Jenny arrived at the A Bar A Ranch. Okay, maybe this wasn't a good idea. As much as she'd tried to stay out of the Raffertys' life, she was smack in the middle of things again. She wanted to blame it on Allison, but she could have made an excuse not to come today. Instead, she'd been looking forward to it.

After climbing out of the car, she headed for the barn as Brian Perkins came out of the corral.

Just a hair under six feet tall, he had that slow, deliberate walk of a man who knew where he was going. His cowboy hat was cocked over his eyes, his sandy hair cut just above his ears.

It had been nearly nine months since she'd last seen him, but it seemed like yesterday. He smiled and lines crinkled around his hazel eyes, showing his forty-plus years. But he still was a handsome devil.

"Hey, pretty girl," he called. "It's good to see you."

She expected that familiar feeling to tighten in her chest, but nothing like that came. She was only glad to see a friend. "Hey, cowboy. You, too."

She was caught off guard when he pulled her into a big hug. "I've missed you."

"That's nice to know."

He released her. "Do you still hate me?"

She blinked at his frankness. "Let's not beat around the bush."

He sobered. "It was never my intention to hurt you."

They'd dated for a few months nearly two summers ago when she'd been working on Allison's cable TV show. It had been pretty intense, but there had always been something missing between them. She had been the one with the forever fantasies. When the breakup came, it had been more pride than her heart being involved. She'd gone back to San Antonio and her teaching job.

"Don't worry, Perkins, I got over you a long time ago. So get over yourself."

He tossed her that grin she'd once been so crazy about, but it didn't affect her the way it used to. Suddenly she realized what Brian had tried to tell her: they were headed in different directions. As a divorced father, he wanted time with his nearly grown kids, and she wanted to start a family.

"I'm wounded." He clutched his chest dramatically. "Was I so easy to forget?"

She fought a smile. "I guess I was, too."

"No way." His gaze locked on her. "I just wasn't the guy for you." Brian reached out and touched her cheek. "There's a lucky man who's gonna win your heart."

Before she could say anything, she heard her name. She turned around to see Gracie running toward her, followed by a stoic-looking Evan Rafferty.

"Hi, Gracie," she said.

She hugged the girl as her father walked up. "Hello, Evan." She glanced over her shoulder, suddenly feeling uneasy. "Brian Perkins, this is Evan Rafferty and his daughter, Gracie. Brian's the ranch foreman and Alex's partner in his cattle business."

The two men exchanged handshakes. "Evan. It's a good day for a ride."

Evan gave a curt nod. "Yeah, it is."

This wasn't going well, Jenny thought, not

knowing why. "Brian and Alex also breed quarter horses." She filled in the silence as the two men stared at each other.

"Rafferty. Is that Rafferty's Vineyard?"

Evan nodded.

Thank goodness, the Casalis were walking toward them, Cherry hurrying on ahead. Her limp was barely noticeable these days. How great was it that a kid could go from a wheelchair to walking in barely two years?

"Morning everyone," Allison called.

"Hi, Mrs. C," Gracie said.

Cherry grabbed the girl's hand and led her toward Alex. "Dad, this is Gracie Rafferty. She's my new friend."

"Hi, Mr. C.," Gracie said shyly. "Thank you for letting me ride with Cherry today."

Smiling, Alex bent down to speak to the child. "It's my pleasure, Gracie. Any friend of Cherry's is always welcome here." He went to the adults and hugged Jenny. "Jenny Collins, it's been far too long between visits. The twins want to know when you're coming to read them stories again."

She liked Alex, especially since he treated his wife like a princess. "I figured since you were outnumbered by women as it was, you didn't need another one giving you trouble."

Alex laughed. "I like that kind of trouble." He looked at Evan. "It's good to see you again, Evan."

"Alex. I appreciate you inviting us. My daughter has been looking forward to this." So was he. The A Bar A Ranch was an incredible operation.

Evan glanced at Jenny beside the foreman, recalling how cozy they'd been earlier. So what? It didn't bother him who her friends were.

"Come on, girls," Alex called. "Let's get our horses."

The giggling twosome held hands all the way into the corral. Allison and Alex hurried after the girls and Jenny fell into step beside Evan. "Do you ride much?" she asked.

"Don't worry, I'll manage to keep up," he told her.

"I only meant that since you work the vineyard, you probably don't have time to ride."

"I've done my share of cowboying over the years." He nodded toward Perkins. "Is your boyfriend going with us?"

Without so much as a glance in his direction, Jenny kept walking. "Probably not." Then she hurried on to catch up with the group.

Evan cursed. Why did it matter if Jenny Collins had a boyfriend? He had no time to care about what she did. Too bad she'd managed to get into his head anyway. How the hell did that happen?

CHAPTER FIVE

EVAN headed for the corral and spotted the line of horses saddled and ready to ride. Today was about spending the afternoon with his daughter.

"That's Cinnamon," Cherry said, pointing at a little chestnut filly. "She's my horse. And there's Speckles for you." Gracie's horse was a small black-and-white paint.

"Oh, she's pretty." Gracie looked back at Evan. "Daddy, is it okay to ride her?"

Evan knew his daughter was far from an expert rider. Brian came up beside the horse. "She's real gentle. I saddle-broke her myself."

"That's reassuring, but I'll be close by to make sure everything will be okay," Evan said.

Brian smiled. "I would do the same if Gracie were mine. Your horse is Diego." He nodded toward a large black gelding. "He'll give you speed if you want, but he's also good on the trail."

"Did you break this one, too?" Evan asked, unable to keep the sarcasm out of his voice.

"I've worked pretty much every horse on this place."

After Evan checked his horse, he found the foreman watching him.

"Since you're wondering," Brian began, "Yes, Jenny and I dated a while back. We're still friends and I care about what happens to her." His gaze locked with Evan. "I wouldn't want to see her hurt. Her family has done enough taking advantage of her, so her friends look out for her."

The meaning was clear and Evan nodded. "Too bad you blew your chance."

After a long stare, the man walked off to help the other riders. Evan let out a breath. Where had that come from? He walked around the animal and checked the cinch. "Hell, I don't have the time or energy to care," he muttered.

Hearing laughter, he glanced at the pretty blonde on her horse. His body stirred as Jenny turned to him and smiled.

"Get moving, Rafferty," she called. "We have places to go." He suddenly realized that everyone was waiting for him.

Gracie waved him on. "Yeah, Daddy, hurry up."

He mounted the horse and moved up with the group. "Okay, what are we waiting for?"

Gracie grinned at him. "It's going to be so much fun."

He felt his chest tighten, realizing his daughter hadn't had much to smile about for a long time. He glanced at Jenny. Maybe he needed some help with that, after all.

About twenty minutes later, they arrived at a creek. The sound of rushing water took them to an ancient oak tree arched over the water's edge, forming a natural canopy. Large rocks and boulders were piled on either side along the winding stream.

Jenny had only been here once before, but she'd never forgotten it. She also knew that this was a special place for Alex and Allison. She glanced at the couple who were whispering between themselves.

She got the funny feeling that she was intruding, remembering all the stumbling blocks that the two had gone through to get to a happy ending. And they were obviously happy.

Would it ever be that way for her? She glanced at Evan. He was helping the girls down, but he caught her gaze. There was definitely something there. Did he feel it, too? No! This was not the man for her. Besides, it was too soon for him, and definitely not the time or place for her.

"Come on, Jenny," Gracie called. "We're going to eat."

She climbed down and walked to the clearing where Allison had spread out a blanket on the ground. Alex brought over two cloth bags that had been tied to his saddle.

"I wonder what Tilda packed for us," he said.

Tilda Emerson had been adopted into the Casali family years ago. The one-time housekeeper and bookkeeper was now Alex's partner in Cherry's Camp for disabled children. Best of all, she was a great cook.

Gracie and Cherry sat down on the blanket. Alex handed a bag to each girl. They found chicken salad and peanut butter sandwiches along with chips, fruit and soft drinks.

Everyone chose a shady spot among the rocks. Jenny watched as they all paired off, leaving her with Evan.

"Relax," Evan said. "I won't bite."

Jenny wasn't sure about that as she took the spot next to him. It was quiet while everyone concentrated on food. The girls giggled over silly things, Alex and Evan talked, trying to skirt any business topics but not doing too well.

"I hear you're still running a cow/calf operation," Alex said.

Evan shrugged. "My plans changed when my brother came back from the army. We're partners for now. He's started a cattle-transport business, too. My main focus is still the vineyard."

"Are you ever going to produce your own label?"

Evan nodded. "Someday."

Jenny could hear the pride in his voice.

Finally Allison stepped in. "Whoa, guys. There's no business, remember?"

Soon the girls finished their sandwiches, then asked permission to go and walk along the edge of the creek.

"Just keep in eyeshot, Cherry," her father said.

Once the girls took off, Alex removed his hat and laid his head on his wife's lap. "This is the life," he sighed.

Listening to the soothing sound of the water, Jenny thought she wouldn't mind a nap, too. She stole a glance at Evan. He wasn't relaxed at all. She wanted to reach out and help ease the tension from his back.

He turned to her. "What's wrong?"

"Nothing."

Soon Alex stood up and reached for his wife's hand. "I think we'll go for a walk." He nodded toward the girls. "We'll be close by."

The couple walked off, but Jenny wanted to call them back. She had a feeling that her friends had planned their departure so she'd be alone with Evan.

"How do you like the view?" she asked.

Evan finally looked at her. "It's nice. Everything about the A Bar A is nice. Of course, when you have money you can have a showplace."

She laughed.

"What's so funny?"

"If you only knew where Alex came from."

"I hear he has family in Italy."

"His mother was American, but she wasn't around much for her twin sons, Alex and Angelo. They pretty much lived on the streets. Alex has gone hungry enough to appreciate the good life. And now he has Allison and the kids."

Evan glanced out at the stream. "Hard work is easy when you have someone to share it with."

Jenny hugged her knees to her chest, hearing the distant tone in Evan's voice. Was he thinking about Megan? Of course he was. They'd loved each other. "It has to be hard to move on after losing the one you shared your dreams with."

He glanced toward the creek. "Sometimes sharing is overrated." He glanced at her. "How serious were you and Perkins?"

Jenny was caught off guard. "Brian? We dated a while back." She knew now that she'd tried to make it more, but Brian had been right, they made better friends. "It ended when I returned to San Antonio."

He looked at her with those deep blue eyes. "You're a teacher."

She nodded. "High-school English."

He grimaced. "Not my favorite class."

"I bet I could have helped change your mind."

His gaze grew intense. "If you'd been my teacher I would have tried harder."

The tremor in his voice caused her to shiver, and she had to look away.

"Why aren't you still in San Antonio?"

"I'm on a leave of absence, but I hope to go back."

"What happened?"

She wasn't ashamed about what had happened. "I felt that one of my students was unfairly expelled and lost a chance for a scholarship. I tangled with the principal, and we both decided I needed some time to regroup."

She felt his heated gaze. "That doesn't surprise me."

"What? That I'm in trouble?"

His mouth quirked at one corner. "No, that you put a kid first."

She shrugged. "It's my job, Evan. Someone has to be on their side."

He touched her hand, his broad fingers moving

over the backs of hers. "Who's on your side, Jenny Collins?"

Between his voice and his touch, she had trouble putting together a thought. "My friends, Allison for one."

"So there's never been anyone special, except Perkins?"

She fought a shiver. "No one worth mentioning. And Brian is still a friend."

Another hint of a smile. "They're all blind then. You're a beautiful woman and distracting as hell."

She laughed trying to keep it light. "You have such a way with words, Rafferty."

"I've never had a way with words."

She doubted that. She also knew she couldn't give this man anything. That didn't mean she didn't want to, but he was too dangerous. "Are you flirting with me?"

Suddenly, he pulled back. Any hint of playfulness was gone. "Just making conversation."

The sound of the girls caused them to turn. Cherry and Gracie came running toward them, followed by Alex and Allison.

Gracie dropped to the blanket. "Daddy, Cherry asked if I can spend the night at her house." The girl took a breath. "We don't have school tomorrow and her mom and dad said I could if it's okay with you." Her blue eyes widened in anticipation. "Please, Daddy."

Jenny could see Evan fighting with an answer. "Are you sure it's okay with her parents?"

Allison appeared. "It's fine. The girls are about the same size, so Gracie can borrow something to wear from Cherry. And I'll bring her home tomorrow morning."

Both girls turned back to Evan, wide-eyed, silently waiting for his answer. He knew Jenny was watching for his reaction, too. He nodded. "Okay, you can stay the night."

Gracie jumped up and down along with Cherry, then she hugged him. "Oh, thank you, Daddy." Just as quickly she released him and returned to her new friend.

"Can we go back now?" Cherry asked. "We want to play in my room."

Alex took charge. "Then let's clean up and get going."

The girls began to pack things in the bags as Alex came up to Evan. "The first time is the toughest," he said. "We want to protect our little girls, and all they want is to be independent." Alex looked at him. "It's no secret you and Gracie have had a rough couple of years. It's good to let her get out on her own."

"She's never wanted to before," Evan admitted.

"Now, she's asking for things I have no idea how to give her."

Alex shook his head. "Females. They're hard to figure out sometimes." He suddenly grinned. "But they sure make life interesting." The man turned and shared a glance with his wife. "Oh, yeah, very interesting."

Evan couldn't stop looking at Jenny as she helped the kids gather things. She must have sensed his gaze because she turned around. When she smiled, a warm heat shot through him, settling low in his gut.

He tore his gaze away and found Alex watching him. "Jenny's a special person with a big heart. I'd hate to see her hurt again."

The message was clear. "I don't plan to hurt her," Evan said, knowing the only way for no one to get hurt was for him to stay away from the woman.

He was going to do his darnedest to accomplish just that.

Later that evening, Evan sat on a stool at Rory's Bar and Grill as his dad worked behind the bar, drawing beers from the tap and mixing drinks. Rory's wasn't usually busy on a Sunday night and Evan was glad. He took a drink of his beer and listened to a Carrie Underwood ballad on the jukebox.

Too restless to sit around the house alone with Gracie gone to the Casalis', he'd surprised himself when he got into his truck and drove into town.

His dad came over. "Can I get you another one?"

Evan stared down at his half-empty glass. "No, I'll nurse this one for a while."

Sean nodded. "You should come around more often."

"I've never been the type to hang out in bars. And I usually have Gracie."

Sean studied his son. "And you were married young, and then Gracie came along."

Yeah, she'd arrived seven months after the wedding. Evan thought back to those days when Megan had returned from college, fresh with her degree and so many dreams.

He'd been working the Merrick Ranch and saving for his own place. They'd dated only a few times before spending the night together. A few months later, with Megan pregnant, they were standing in front of a preacher. After Gracie's birth they'd moved into the foreman's cottage at her parents' vineyard.

"Socializing seemed to get me into trouble."

His father smiled. "I think you're older and

wiser now. Besides, you can't regret that beautiful child."

"I regret a lot, but never her. She's the reason I'm working so much. I know I don't show her the love I should, but it's hard."

Sean placed his hands on the bar. "And I don't like to speak ill of the dead, son, but Megan didn't help you bond with your daughter."

Evan took a long drink of his beer. He didn't want to rehash the past. "Maybe if things had been different…" He knew that he had tried to get close to his wife. Maybe if they had been head over heels in love to start with they could have worked harder at being a couple, a family. He'd tried, but Megan was unreceptive to the idea.

"You can't change the past, Evan," his father continued. "So it's time to move on. Don't give up on finding someone else."

"What I need is to concentrate on Gracie."

"A loving relationship with a woman would be good for your daughter. You're only thirty-three. It's a normal thing to want to be with a woman."

He really didn't want to hear this. "Didn't we have this conversation when I was thirteen?"

Sean laughed. "You didn't listen then either." His smile faded. "Just don't give up on making a life for yourself, son."

He met his father's gaze. "How come you never found anyone after Mom left us?"

Sean shrugged. "I guess I wasn't looking, or there wasn't the opportunity." He glanced to the doorway. "Not like you." A slow smile creased his face. "How lucky can you get when that special one walks in the door?"

Evan turned his head and found Jenny standing at the entrance. He didn't need her here. He didn't need his heart racing, or his gut tightening into knots at the sight of her, either. Yet lately that seemed to be a common occurrence whenever she was around.

That meant big trouble for him.

Jenny had called herself crazy as she changed out of her comfortable sweats and into a pair of jeans and a cotton T-shirt. Then again when she slipped on a pair of heeled sandals and hurried down the steps of her apartment and out the back of the shop.

She told herself she was wanting a barbecue sandwich and some fries. That was her story and she was sticking to it. Spotting the Rafferty ranch truck from her window had nothing to do with it.

Telling herself she needed to stay away from Evan hadn't slowed her progress as she crossed the nearly deserted street toward the neon sign of Rory's Bar and Grill. She took a breath, and walked into the dimly lit room.

A wooden L-shaped bar ran nearly the length of the space. Against the side walls were a half dozen high-backed booths, mostly empty tonight. It was a nice place with a warm atmosphere.

"Hi," she said, too breathless. Evan looked good, freshly shaved and wearing a starched Western shirt and nice jeans.

He nodded. "Jenny."

She glanced away. "Hello, Sean," she called as the older man came around the bar to greet her with a hug.

"Hi, lass. You look mighty pretty tonight."

She couldn't even remember if she'd put on any makeup. "Thank you."

"So you finally decided to check the place out?"

"My own cooking brought me here. I hear you serve a great barbecue sandwich."

Sean winked at her. "It's the best. What else can I get you?"

"Some fries and make it to go."

Sean frowned. "You can't go home and eat alone." He glanced at his son. "Evan was about to eat. Go and sit in a booth. Share some conversation and I'll bring you your food. What do you want to drink?"

Jenny wasn't sure this was a good idea. "I'll have whatever Evan's drinking."

Sean hurried off, and she heard Evan say, "We'd better do as he says. You're not getting out of here until you eat."

"I didn't intend to interrupt your evening." She was such a lousy liar, but he didn't look too happy to see her. "I mean, you don't have to babysit me."

"Have you heard me complain?" He led her to a booth and she scooted in.

"I'll be right back," he said and went behind the bar to draw a beer from the tap. He walked back and set both glasses on the table, then slid next to her.

She took a sip of beer. "Okay, Rafferty. Is this how you spend your night off?" She knew Gracie was sleeping over at the Casalis'.

"Geez, do you think I'm out chasing women?" He turned toward her, giving a hint of a smile. "Sorry to disappoint, but I'd rather have a quiet evening, enjoying a drink and talking with my dad."

She nodded. "Being single sucks, huh?"

He locked those baby blues on her. "From where I'm sitting it doesn't look so bad."

She felt a warm shiver go through her. "Oh, I bet you say that to all the ladies."

"This is Kerry Springs, not San Antonio. A social life is pretty limited."

"I'm sure you draw the attention of a lot of females in this town."

He took a long drink from his mug. "You've mistaken me for Matt. I don't go out much."

She sobered when reality hit. "You still miss your wife."

He didn't acknowledge her statement. "My concern is Gracie. We hadn't exactly been close. Not like she and her mother were."

Jenny toyed with her glass, envying any relationship between a mother and daughter. "And you've been working on that. You've helped her get to class."

"And you've talked me into letting her have a sleepover, which you're helping with. You must have caught me at a weak moment." He turned to her. "Thanks for volunteering to help."

"Hold the applause and wait until we see if it's a success," she smiled.

He nodded, his long tapered fingers rubbing up and down the sides of the beer glass. "There's something else I want to get off my chest."

She watched him. No other man had ever made her so aware of her femininity with just one look. He was a big man, but there was softness to his strength. She could easily slip into his arms. She shook it off and said, "What is that?"

"I apologize for nosing into your business with Perkins. I had no right."

She blinked in surprise. "Accepted. And for the record, only in my head did our relationship get serious." She met his gaze. "Brian is a nice guy. I think I fell more for the idea of love than I actually fell in love."

He held her gaze. "It can be incredible, I hear."

She caught a flicker of something in his eyes. Regret. Loneliness. Was he saying his marriage wasn't as perfect as people had believed it to be?

She glanced away. No, this wasn't any of her business. "You have Gracie and your family."

He sighed. "Yeah. A nosy father and a pushy brother. Whom you need to watch out for. Matt can be pretty charming."

She doubted Matt was the Rafferty she had to worry about. She fought a smile. "I'll keep that in mind."

Before he could speak, Sean carried out two large plates of food and placed them down on the table.

"Sorry it took so long." He placed his hands on his hips and grinned. "Nothing like good food and conversation," he said as a lone customer walked in the door. "Got to get to work." He waved as he went behind the bar. "Hello, Michael."

Suddenly Evan was feeling like a teenager. He was far too aware of the woman beside him. The more time he spent with Jenny the more he felt he wanted her. Question was, did he want to do anything about it?

"This smells delicious," she said.

"Dad wasn't lying when he said it's the best around."

He watched as Jenny picked up her oversized sandwich and took a bite, leaving a smear of sauce on the side of her mouth. Desire shot through him as he fought the urge to lean forward and remove it, giving both a taste. Instead he picked up a napkin.

"Here, you have sauce on your mouth." He reached out and wiped it off. She froze, allowing him to clean her up. Their eyes locked and instantly he was mesmerized. "Damn, woman," he breathed, then pulled away. "Eat your food before we both get into trouble."

Twenty minutes later they'd finished the meal.

"I can't finish all this," Jenny announced, leaving half her food. "I'm stuffed."

Evan patted his stomach. "I didn't have any trouble." He hadn't realized how hungry he was. And not only for food. He looked at Jenny. Although he didn't want to leave her, the direction his thoughts were taking wasn't a good idea.

"I hate to cut this short," he began, "but I need to get up early tomorrow. I'm helping Matt move cattle."

She groaned. "I think they should outlaw Mondays. But if truth be told, I'd probably get up early anyway. I love dawn."

Evan stood. "It's my favorite time, too." He placed some bills on the table, but when she reached for her wallet he stopped her. "Don't even think about it."

"But you don't need to pay for my supper."

"What if I want to?" He helped her out of the booth. "What if I wanted to share dinner and conversation with you?"

Her gaze held his. "I just didn't want you to feel you had to."

"If I'd felt that way, I'd have let you take your food back to your apartment. Can we agree sharing a meal was nice?"

She nodded. "Yes, nice," she said in a soft, breathy voice.

"Now, hopefully without argument, I'm going to walk you home."

Jenny nodded, then they waved to Sean and headed for the door. He followed her out into the darkness, then took her by the elbow as they crossed the street. It was dark as they made their way to the other side and started down the alley. Several sensor lights came on as they walked past the other businesses on the way to the back door of the quilt shop.

"It was a nice evening, Rafferty. Thank you."

She took out her keys, but he stopped her. "I like it when you call me Evan." He knew in his head this was a bad idea, but couldn't stop himself as he pulled her toward him. He gave her a chance to back away, but she didn't. "Say my name, Jenny."

She swallowed. "Evan," she breathed, and his mouth closed over hers.

Evan shut everything out of his mind, except for the feel of Jenny's body pressed against his. He drew a breath and inhaled her fresh scent. He reached up and cupped her head, feeling the silkiness of her hair. On a soft moan, she opened her mouth and he got to taste her intoxicating sweetness. He hadn't realized how hungry she made him.

He broke off the kiss but not his hold.

"Maybe this isn't a good idea," Jenny breathed as her arms slipped around his neck.

His mouth brushed over hers; he wasn't listening at all to common sense. "It feels pretty damn good to me."

CHAPTER SIX

It was a little before nine the following morning when Jenny came downstairs to the shop. Millie was already there, and, to her surprise, so were several other women. They were all seated at the round table at the window.

"What's going on?" Jenny asked as she came up next to her coworker.

Millie took her to the table. "Meet the ladies of the Quilters' Corner. You already know Beth Staley and this is Louisa Merrick and Liz Parker. And soon there will be more."

Jenny smiled, excited they were here. "Morning, ladies. I'm glad you're taking advantage of the space."

Millie turned to her. "You know, most times when you get a bunch of women together there's drama."

"There's just going to be quilting," Louisa Merrick said. She was an attractive woman in her late fifties. Her raven hair was laced with gray and pulled into a bun, showing off her beautiful bone structure. Her dark eyes sparkled. "My husband, Clay, is a Texas politician. He causes enough drama."

Everyone laughed.

"Sounds like your life is exciting," Jenny said, knowing a little of Senator Merrick's reputation.

Louisa smiled. "I'd rather have a houseful of grandkids to spoil, but my son, Sloan, is a little slow to fill my request." Louisa smiled. "You say you're single?"

Jenny found herself stuttering. *Please don't let anyone set me up with a date.*

Beth spoke up. "Sloan is more interested in raising his free-range cattle than in women right now. Jenny's been busy, too…with her girls' class."

"He'll be interested," Louisa assured her, "when he finds the right woman." She looked encouragingly at Jenny.

"I won't be staying in town past the summer. I'll be returning to San Antonio and my teaching job."

After a series of groans from the women, Beth started talking about her granddaughter, Kasey. And Jenny was happy to no longer be the main topic of discussion. What would everyone think if they knew Evan Rafferty had kissed the daylights out of her last night?

She smiled to herself, knowing that, as much as she'd enjoyed the kiss, she couldn't make too much out of it. Talk about a mismatch. Evan wasn't the man for her. A warm shiver went through her at the memory of his touch.

Maybe if she wrote it on a piece of paper a hundred times then she'd start to believe it.

That same morning, Evan began his day as usual. He walked through the vines, checking the grapes as he had every day for years. He'd always been a man who thrived on routine, on habit.

But he wasn't in the habit of kissing women.

He closed his eyes and Jenny came to mind. In the last twelve hours he hadn't been able to erase her image, or the feel of her against him, or the taste of her.

The truth was, kissing Jenny had been incredible. He hadn't wanted to stop, but he'd had to. It wasn't wrong to want a woman, he told himself, especially a woman as appealing as the dark-eyed blonde.

What bothered him was how she made him feel. He wanted casual, and she had marriage and kids written all over her. He couldn't go there again. Besides, Jenny had befriended his daughter. That could complicate things all to hell. And he needed to put his energy into his relationship with Gracie.

No, marriage wasn't for him. He couldn't make his first one work, so why would he try again?

At the sound of a horn, he looked over his shoulder and saw a crew-cab truck pull up next to the barn. Alex Casali and Gracie got out along with her new friend, Cherry. His daughter waved and he started down the slope as the group came toward him.

"Hey, Gracie." He'd missed her more than he could have imagined.

"Hi, Daddy," she called, surprising him as she rushed into his arms.

"Did you have a good time?"

She stood back and smiled. "It was so much fun. We watched movies and played video games."

Hadn't she missed him at all? "Sounds like fun to me."

"Daddy, when can I have my sleepover?"

"I'm not exactly sure." He glanced at Alex. "We need to discuss that with Jenny."

Gracie looked at Cherry. "Jenny's going to be the woman in the house. Daddy says mothers won't let their girls come with only men here."

Alex hid a grin. "Wise idea."

Gracie turned back to Evan. "Will you ask her?"

He wasn't sure he was ready to face Jenny yet. "Okay."

"Today?"

That could be an excuse to see her again. "We'll see."

Gracie looked at her new friend. "Come on, I want to show you my room."

"Ten minutes, Cherry," Alex called after the twosome running toward the house. "Then we need to leave." He turned back to Evan. "I doubt she even heard me." He nodded toward the vine-yard. "How about showing me around?"

Evan was surprised by the request. "Sure."

Together they walked toward the rows of vines, heavy with grapes. "It's quiet now, but we'll start harvesting in a few months," Evan said. "We'll be busy then."

"How many acres planted?"

"Right now it's about twelve."

Alex studied him. "You have plans for more?"

Evan turned away. "I've always had plans for more. Just not in the near future."

"You sell to Solomon Creek Winery?"

Evan nodded. "Yes, my pinot grigio grapes." He pointed to the highest section of the hill. "They're harvested first. Then zinfandel and muscat. They're all my grapes, but under his label."

"I'm impressed."

Evan was surprised. "Why? You've done well in the cattle business, and it's been a lot more profitable."

"Success is not always measured by financial gain." Alex smiled. "I discovered that when I met Allison and Cherry." There was a long pause. "You've had a rough few years, but you've come through it."

Evan didn't want to go there. "I have a daughter to think about now." He glanced around the vineyard. "This is for her. It's her heritage."

"Is she the reason you wanted to build the winery?"

"That was part of the Kerchers' plan, then my wife's. Now, it's the Rafferty Vineyard. I'm more into growing the grapes. And they're in demand as the hill-country wine business grows. These wineries here are winning awards all over the world."

"You're quite the spokesperson."

"It is my livelihood."

They stopped at the crest of the hill. "What's your dream?"

"It's pretty simple—to grow the best grapes and run my own label." Evan just wasn't sure he could pull it off by himself. Although his brother helped out, Matt was more interested in the cattle operation.

Alex studied him. "The important thing is to have a dream. That was my problem for years." Alex raised an eyebrow. "I worried too much about accomplishing things, making money, moving on to the next step, so that I couldn't enjoy what I had. It's important to have someone to share it with."

Evan had to agree, but he had a feeling Alex Casali wasn't talking about sharing all this with Gracie, but with another female.

Jenny rolled over in bed and glanced at the clock on her nightstand—6:55 a.m. Since it was only five minutes until the alarm would go off she might as well get up. Sitting on the edge of the bed, her thoughts flashed to Evan. It had been two days since she'd been foolish enough to let things go so far.

Big mistake. She never should have gone to Rory's. Never should have let Evan kiss her. What had made her think they could be just friends?

She released a breath and walked out of her bedroom and into the main room of the apartment.

The newly remodeled attic space that had once belonged to Allison was smaller than Jenny's place in San Antonio, but she didn't have to share it with a roommate.

She walked over to the compact kitchen with its new cabinets and appliances, not that she needed more than a microwave. She took a diet soda from the refrigerator, popped the tab and went into the living area. Bamboo floors were covered by a sisal rug, and a grass-green love seat and two tan leather chairs faced the small flat-screen television banked on either side with floor-to-ceiling bookcases. There wasn't any wasted space here.

It was fine, temporarily, but her goal was to go back to San Antonio and her teaching job at the high school. Not to kiss a cowboy/vineyard owner. That had been what had got her into trouble two summers ago with Brian. She brushed her hair away from her face and took a gulp of the caffeine-charged drink. She needed a clear head. She didn't need to fantasize about Evan Rafferty's arms around her, his mouth against hers, sending incredible feelings through her.

No! No! No!

She wasn't ready for this man. More importantly, Rafferty wasn't ready for her. He had a wife that he hadn't put to rest, a daughter he was trying to parent. Her heart tightened at the thought of Gracie. How blessed she would be to have a sweet little girl like her.

She shook her head. "You're dreaming again, Jen."

Once again she heard the familiar words. Marsha Collins-Newsome had always been a realist. She hadn't believed in dreams. A single mother beaten down by life, she'd married the first guy who could give her a decent home. Carl Newsome, a widower with three wild sons: Carl Junior, Mike and Todd. The boys were older than Jenny, and they'd spent their adolescence making things difficult for her. The youngest son, Todd, had been the worst. He'd made her life a living hell, and even as adults he wouldn't leave her alone. She was glad he'd been sent to prison and hoped that she never had to see him again. No, the Newsomes and Collinses had never quite managed to become a nurturing family. The furthest thing from it.

Jenny remembered her visit with the Raffertys. They weren't perfect, but they cared about each other. Her chest tightened with that same old longing. She wanted what she'd never had. A loving family.

She turned her thoughts back to Evan. He wasn't the man for her. Too much baggage, and she didn't want to be the rebound girl.

The only stability in her life had been her teaching. Since college, it had filled a lot of empty places. She needed to get back to it. And nothing was going to stop her.

Not even the good-looking Evan Rafferty.

Later that day, Jenny had just finished with a customer when the bell over the door rang and Evan walked in. Her heart began to race. She hated that she reacted to the man.

Evan removed his hat and nodded to Beth Staley.

The older woman stopped and talked with him a moment, then he held the door open for her and she walked out.

He made his way across the store. Those deep-blue eyes locked in on Jenny. She felt her breathing speed up. She had to stop this. This wasn't high school.

"Jenny," he said as he stopped at the other side of the counter.

"Rafferty," she returned, not seeing a bit of uneasiness in him. "What can I do for you?"

He glanced around, hearing voices from the tables in the classroom area. "Can we talk?"

Dear Lord, no. She didn't want to hear that he was sorry he kissed her. "I'm rather busy right now."

He held his hat in his hand. "When will you have time?"

Millie suddenly appeared. "I can watch things for a while." She smiled at Evan. "You could go back to the office."

Evan nodded to her. "Thank you." Then without any warning, he came around the counter and took Jenny by the arm and walked her toward the back of the store. Inside the small office she stopped in front of the file cabinet, but when she turned around, she found Evan right there. His gaze was intense, his scent engulfed her.

"What's so important?" she managed.

"I need to know if you still plan to chaperone Gracie's sleepover."

She was almost relieved that was the reason he'd stopped by. "Yes, I promised her that I would. Why? Have you changed your mind?"

He studied her for a moment, then shook his head. "I was thinking you might have after what happened the other night."

Now she saw his uneasiness. It was endearing, but she couldn't let him get to her. "Get over yourself, Rafferty. It was only a kiss." One that had nearly knocked her socks off, she added silently.

He leaned in closer. She could feel his breath warm against her face. Then he grinned. He wasn't playing fair. "Glad you feel that way." He stepped back. "Because the invitations went out for Friday night."

She worked to clear the dryness from her throat. "What invitations?"

"The sleepover at my house," he said.

She knew he was talking about Gracie's party, but suddenly a picture of Evan and her in a big bed flashed through her head. Whoa. She blinked and turned away. "What time?"

"Gracie told her friends seven o'clock. Maybe you could come by a little early, and don't be surprised if Matt and Dad have some surprises planned."

Jenny found it easy to smile. That was just like those two. "Sounds like fun."

He grumbled something. "I just want to survive the night."

She laughed. "Buck up, fella, this is only the beginning."

"That's what I'm afraid of."

Friday night arrived, along with a half dozen screaming girls and their thundering footsteps overhead in Gracie's bedroom.

"Saints save us," his father said, looking up at the ceiling. "What in the world are they doing up there?"

"I don't know. I only hope the house is still standing in the morning," Evan replied, shrugging. "Of course, Jenny's up there supervising." Then came another thud. "Maybe they tied her up and put her in a closet."

Sean laughed. "That's something you and your brother would have done. But if it happens, then you can go up and save the pretty lass."

And who would save him? he wondered. Once the girls had found out Jenny was going to be there tonight they were even more excited to come. For him, having her in the house seemed strange, but to everyone else, she fitted in. She did fit in. Maybe that was the problem.

The sound of little girls' voices grew louder, and then came the stampede of footsteps on the stairs.

"Brace yourselves, here they come," Sean said.

One by one, three little blondes, two brunettes and one red-haired girl arrived in the kitchen. Every one of them had big hair and tons of makeup on those sweet angelic faces.

Gracie proudly climbed up on a bar stool. The other girls followed her. "Hi, Daddy. We're having a lot of fun."

"I can see that." He looked her over, trying to find his little girl under all the makeup. "Trying a new look?"

"Oh, Daddy. We're doing the eighties. You know, Madonna, Bon Jovi. ABBA, too."

The other girls broke into a chorus of "Dancing Queen," then fell into a fit of giggles.

"Daddy, did you know Jenny can moonwalk like Michael Jackson?

"No, I didn't." Evan looked at his dad and mouthed, "Madonna."

Sean shrugged and whispered, "I'm sure Jenny has it under control."

"All the girls think Jenny is *way* cool. She says we're going to work our way through the decades.

We'll finish with Hannah Montana and Taylor Swift."

Evan turned back in time to see Jenny walk in. Her hair was big, too, lying in waves past her shoulders. She wore heavy makeup, overdone on the eyes and lips, and some kind of tight stretchy pants that hugged her long sexy legs.

"Hey, girls." She winked at Evan as she sat down on a stool. "Did you get something to eat?" She glanced at his father. "Hi, Sean."

"Hello, young ones," he greeted as he eyed all the girls. "Looks as if I have several customers here." He leaned on the counter. "What can I get for all of you? Pizza? Chips? Ice cream? Hamburgers?"

After the girls placed their orders, the group got up and headed upstairs. Gracie stayed back and said to her father, "Don't come in, because it's for girls only."

Evan nodded. "Okay. We'll knock on the door, then leave the food in the hall."

She kissed him. "Thanks, Daddy." She took off to find the others. The music started up again along with a thumping sound. Evan glanced at the clock to see it was only nine o'clock. Just twelve more hours and they'd all go home. That included Jenny.

* * *

It was midnight and the girls showed no signs of slowing down, but Jenny was running out of ideas for things to do. They didn't want to watch any more videos, or eat any more food. They were too far out in the country for a scavenger hunt. Maybe some scary stories.

She got the girls' attention and started telling tales she remembered from school when something hit against the window.

The girls jumped and gasped. "What was that?" one of them asked.

Jenny got up, pulled the curtains back and looked out the second-story window. Down below a flash of white caught her eyes. "What the…" she began, when she saw the figure standing in the yard. It was Sean. She opened the window and the girls came to see what was going on.

"Sean? Is something wrong?"

"Sorry to disturb you, but I'm looking for some little ones who'd be interested in roasting some marshmallows by the campfire. Maybe tell a few stories."

"We are," the chorus of girls cheered.

"I'm too scared," Carrie said, looking out into the darkness.

"Come on," Cherry said. "Mr. Sean won't let anything happen to us."

"How about if we all go together?" Jenny suggested. "It'll be fun."

"We'll be right down," she called to Sean.

"Good." He smiled. "Bring Evan, too. He's taking a nap before the next shift."

Already dressed in their pajamas, the girls all put on sweatshirts and shoes, then headed down.

Jenny was bringing up the rear when she stopped by the master bedroom. She knocked softly and pushed open the partly closed door to find Evan lying on the bed fully dressed, minus his boots. The lamp beside the bed was on and she could see he was asleep.

"Evan," she whispered, but when he didn't answer, she walked in and stood next to the bed. She stared down at the man lying on the bed. He looked so peaceful, so unlike the Evan who was usually frowning.

She heard the girls at the foot of the stairs and reached out and touched his arm. The warmth of his skin caused her to bite back a gasp.

His eyes shot open, and he quickly sat up. "What happened?"

"Nothing yet. We're going down to roast marshmallows. Your dad said to wake you up."

Her hand was still on his arm. "Sorry, I was catching a few hours sleep." He rubbed his eyes. "What are the munchkins up to now?"

She tried but couldn't seem to move away. "Sean's going to tell stories out by a campfire."

Evan stood up, and she started to back away, but he pulled her closer.

"Rafferty...this isn't a good idea," she warned.

"You're damn right it isn't." He started to lower his head when off in the distance she heard her name.

She quickly broke away, but Evan refused to release her as he held her head against his shoulder. "Kids can be a pain sometimes. This is definitely one of those times."

"Evan...I've got to go. The girls will come looking for me."

With a nod, Evan let her go. He turned and went into the adjoining bathroom and closed the door. She worked to slow her breathing as she walked out and down the steps.

"Jenny," Gracie said, "Where were you? Everybody is waiting."

"I forgot something." She'd forgotten something all right, her mind, her common sense. She looked down at the smiling child and thought about the man upstairs.

She was quickly losing her heart to both of them.

"They're called the wee people. Some call them leprechauns. I only met one, Finn O'Donovan.

And oh, he was a tricky one. He would rob you blind if you turned your back on him."

"What does he look like?" a girl asked.

"A wee man, no bigger than yourselves. They have rosy cheeks and big blue eyes that make you want to trust them. I met Finn when I was no older than you young ones. He lived in the forest right outside of the town where I lived in Ireland. First time I saw him was when I came home from school one day. He asked me never to tell anyone about him. My first mistake. He promised to show me where he hid a pot of gold. Well, let me tell you. I was a poor fella with lots of brothers and sisters. My da and ma could use a pot of gold."

"Did you ever find it?" Carrie asked.

Sean shook his head. "No. The scoundrel had been laughing at me the whole time. Soon after, my family left for America, so I never saw Finn again which was good, since we didn't part on happy terms. But some strange things have been happening lately. I have a feeling that Finn has returned to my life."

"He's here?" Cherry whispered.

Sean's eyes grew large as he nodded, then glanced around the crackling fire at his attentive audience. "I have proof." He reached behind him and pulled out a green felt pointy hat. "See, this is the same hat Finn wore all those years ago."

"Where'd you get that, Grandpa?" Gracie asked.

"I found it in the vineyard. Finn is here."

Everyone gasped.

Evan stood at the patio door and watched as the girls listened to his father. No one could tell a story like Sean Rafferty. Seeing Gracie's happy face, he was glad that his dad was there to help out. His gaze settled on Jenny. This night for Gracie wouldn't have happened if she hadn't agreed to give up her weekend.

The only problem was that it was getting harder and harder to keep away from her. He still couldn't believe what had nearly happened upstairs. He'd almost kissed her again. He wanted it more than his next breath.

Suddenly Matt came out of the shadows, sat on the bench next to Jenny and scooted closer to her. He didn't seem to have any trouble talking with her, flirting with her.

And unless Evan spoke up, he didn't have any right to tell his brother to stay away.

Was he ready to do that?

CHAPTER SEVEN

A WEEK had passed since the sleepover and Jenny had tried to stay focused on other things besides the man who'd been keeping her up nights. Not only Evan had been disturbing her sleep, but worry over his daughter's feelings had, as well.

Classes had been going well for everyone except Gracie. She struggled with the intricate work needed to complete her mother's quilt. Jenny herself even needed Allison's help. The pattern was far too complicated for an eight year old, and the child's frustration was growing.

She'd realized she had to convince the girl to go in another direction. That was when she'd asked for advice from Allison and her new friend, school principal Lily Perry.

The three of them had discussed her concerns and had come up with something that might convince Gracie to put her mother's quilt aside for another few years and work on something simpler.

It was nearly the end of the day's class when

Jenny took Gracie aside. They walked to the round table in the corner of the room that had quickly become a popular spot with the regulars. Only on Wednesday and Saturday afternoons was the area vacant.

Jenny motioned to a chair and Gracie took it. "Am I in trouble?" she asked.

"Of course not." Jenny looked at Allison who'd followed them over. "We just have an idea we want to talk to you about."

The child still looked worried as Jenny took a seat next to her. "I'm concerned about you, Gracie. I think the quilt you're working on is harder than you thought it would be, huh?"

The girl looked sad. "It's not too bad."

Jenny exchanged a glance with Allison. "But still, it's pretty hard to sew for someone your age."

"Maybe."

Jenny was relieved. "Allison and I came up with an idea that might help. We want you to listen to it first, before you decide if it's good or bad."

"Okay."

"We were wondering if you'd consider putting your quilt aside for a few years until you're older and a more experienced quilter."

Tears welled in her eyes. "But I promised Mommy."

"We know you did, sweetie," Jenny said soothingly. "But, as I said before, I don't think your mother expected you to finish it right away. Since she chose the Double-Wedding-Ring pattern, don't you think she planned to have it ready for when you got married?" Jenny smiled. "Are you getting married anytime soon?"

Gracie actually smiled too. "No!"

"Then you have plenty of time to get it done."

"I guess so," she hesitated. "But will you still help me?"

Jenny wasn't sure how to answer her. She'd always planned to go back to San Antonio to teach. "I'll promise you this, Gracie, I'll do my best."

The girl wasn't excited by her answer. "You said you'd help me finish it."

"And if possible, I will. Besides, if you keep practicing, just think how good you'll get and you can do it yourself."

The child looked sad. "Does this mean I can't be in the class any more?"

"Oh, no. We want you to stay in the class. Would you be willing to work on another project, something simpler?"

Gracie nodded eagerly.

"Good. We've come up with an idea and all you girls can work together. Even Mrs. Perry is going to participate in this project." Jenny stood.

"Come on, I'll announce to everyone what's going to happen."

Gracie hurried back to her seat as Jenny turned to Allison. "She took it better than I thought."

"She seemed relieved."

But Jenny wasn't sure she was out of the woods yet. Hadn't she been the one who had fought to get Gracie into class, assuring Evan she could handle it?

Why should she care what he thought? The man had run hot and cold, kissing her, making her want more. But she hadn't seen or heard from him since. Apparently he'd wanted to put some distance between them.

She could deal with rejection. If only he would stay away, stop making her long for more, making her want what she couldn't have—a man who would never be hers.

Jenny walked back to the group. "Girls, it's about quitting time and I'd like to talk to you all."

They stopped and looked at her.

"First of all, I want to tell you how pleased I am with the work you've all accomplished in just a few short weeks." She looked around. "Is everyone having fun?"

The group cheered and Jenny's chest swelled. She glanced at Lily. "Well, if you like what you're doing, we'd like to go a step further. When the class began, we talked about everyone making their own quilt, but that's a big project, and it can take a long time, especially with schoolwork and chores at home. How about we each work on a section of blocks, then everyone combines them to make one quilt?" She rushed on to say, "It'll still be about your family, but we'll put everyone's together."

There was silence.

She continued, "Why not make a quilt that tells a story about the town, about past generations? You are the future of Kerry Springs, but we should know where we came from, too. I know a lot of you are already using fabric from your relatives. That's perfect. Now with the assistance of mothers and the helpers, you can embroider those people's names and dates on the blocks so we'll know who they are." Jenny moved aside so Lily could join her. "And now Mrs. Perry is going to tell you more about this project."

"Hello, girls."

"Hello, Mrs. Perry," they said in unison.

"I'm also impressed with the work you're doing here. And I'm taking a personal interest in this project, since both my daughter and my mother are working on it, too.

"When I first heard of Jenny's idea, I thought, what a great idea, to preserve our town's history in a quilt. And then I thought, as well as a quilt, how about an essay contest? We have Founders' Day coming up in July. So what better way to celebrate it than to write about the families that make our town great?"

Jenny watched as the girls took in the idea.

"This isn't a school requirement. It's strictly for this class and for your own curiosity. But the girls who turn in stories will have them published in the town paper. Even better, Jenny and Allison will display the finished quilt in the shop window so everyone in town will see your hard work." Lily smiled. "How do you feel about that?"

The girls cheered. "We should do it," Cherry said. It was seconded by girl after girl.

"Okay, that gives us three months to finish. So you'll keep working in class, but you'll need to interview your parents and grandparents, learn their stories. Good luck to all of you."

The room buzzed with excitement as the girls put away their sewing while discussing what they were going to do. Jenny glanced toward the back of the room and saw Evan.

Now it was her job to get him to go along with the sudden change of plans.

Evan watched as Jenny moved around the room talking to each student. It was obvious the girls adored her. She had an ease around kids, around everyone.

Not him. Outside of family, he'd always had trouble talking to people. He'd rather be alone than in a group. Megan hadn't been eager to bring him out. She'd had her own social groups; besides quilting, there was her work at the church. Yet now, he could see his daughter needed more.

Although he'd once loved the solitude of working the vineyard, he'd found of late he was lonely. More so when he thought about Jenny Collins. Whenever he got close to her, he could feel the pull. Then there was the memory of the sweetest kiss and the stirring in his body that told him he wanted more, needed more as well.

His daughter came running toward him. "Daddy, guess what?"

"What?"

"We're all going to make a big quilt together and have a writing contest. I need to get some old clothes from Grandpa for my blocks 'cause I'm gonna write about him being from Ireland, and you and Uncle Matt, too."

He looked at Jenny, who had arrived next to his daughter. "So you're working on a new project already?"

"We're taking a little detour," Jenny answered.

Allison and Cherry walked up. "How about us

girls go for some ice cream, Gracie? Then your dad and Jenny can talk."

"Can I go, Daddy?"

Evan dug into his pocket for a few dollars and handed them to her. "Sure, but only get one scoop and don't take too long."

He watched as they left the shop, then turned back to Jenny. "What's going on?"

"First of all, I was planning to tell to you about it when you got here."

"Well, I'm here." He glanced at Millie, who was with a customer. Both ladies were watching them with interest. "Is there somewhere private we can talk?" he asked.

"I can't leave Millie."

"I'll be fine," the saleswoman assured her. "You two go talk." She smiled at Evan. "Good to see you again, Evan. Say hello to your father for me."

He nodded. "I'll do that." He followed Jenny toward the back of the shop. She went to the office, then bypassed it. "The bookkeeper is working in there."

Evan was surprised when Jenny opened another door that led to a staircase and started up. He followed her, and they ended up in her apartment.

He looked around, and then walked to the narrow window. "You can see Main Street."

"Yeah, the view sold me on the place."

He turned his attention to her. She looked tempting in fitted jeans and a tapered green blouse. Her sunny hair hung around her face and thin bangs brushed her forehead, highlighting her big brown eyes. She didn't wear much makeup, giving her a fresh-scrubbed look. His gaze went to her full mouth and her perfect lips.

He shook away the direction of his thoughts. "Okay, what's this change of plans?"

She blew out a breath. "You were right."

He didn't expect her to say that. "About what?"

"Gracie *is* too young to handle the complicated quilt pattern."

He folded his arms across his chest. "Isn't that what I tried to tell you from the beginning?"

"You did," she conceded. "But what you didn't realize about your daughter was she needed some independence. And she had to attempt to do the quilt before anyone could convince her otherwise. It seems stubbornness runs in your family."

"You think I'm stubborn? You're the one who wouldn't let go of this."

"But it helped. Can't you see the difference in her?"

He nodded. "All right. She has been happier these last few weeks. But she has to be disappointed that she can't finish the quilt."

Jenny shook her head. "Oh, she'll finish it, but

she's willing to wait." She smiled. "And she got the one thing she truly wanted."

"What was that?"

"Your attention."

"She's always had my attention," he said.

"On your terms. The only outlet she had was school."

"We live in the country."

"But your daughter is growing up, she needs to socialize. And this class has helped her."

Had he been that selfish? "Don't forget I let her have a sleepover. But I'll always want to protect her no matter how old she gets."

"Of course, and she'll always need that from you, along with your love."

"She's always had that, from the day she was born." Evan felt the familiar sadness. "I never want her to ever doubt that." He walked away then turned back to Jenny. "There were days when that little girl was the only reason I got out of bed. She kept me going."

Jenny nodded, trying not to reach out and offer comfort to this man. She was already too involved. "And you helped your daughter get through losing her mother. She wants to help you, too. She knows how sad you've been."

His blue eyes met hers. "You seem to know a lot about her."

Jenny shrugged. "I was a stranger when she first talked to me. That made it easier for her."

"You are easy to talk to. Thank you for spending time with Gracie, especially for last weekend's sleepover."

That was her, the person everyone wanted to share things with, to be friends with. Last weekend, when Evan had nearly kissed her again, she'd known it was a bad idea. She'd already gotten a taste of his loving family, something she'd always longed for, giving her ideas of having a piece of it.

"That might have created more problems." She held his gaze as it did crazy things to her stomach, but she continued. "It changes things now, Rafferty, we might never be able to go back. You aren't ready."

"For what? To kiss you again? Hell, yes, I'm ready." He was more than ready for her. He moved closer, stopping directly in front of her. He caught her scent. It was intoxicating. Feelings for her whirled in his head. "If you're honest, Jenny, you'd admit you want it too."

"That doesn't make it the right thing to do."

"No, it doesn't." He leaned toward her. "All my energy needs to go into keeping the ranch afloat and being a father to my daughter." He released a breath. "But you're the one I've been thinking about in the middle of the night. You're the one I want to hold in my arms, want to kiss—"

She looked up at the ceiling. "Oh, Rafferty, why are you doing this to me? We're headed in different directions. Starting anything would be foolish."

Hell, he didn't want to get involved, but it had already happened. "Yeah, you're right about that. It would be the craziest thing ever."

"For once we agree." Her voice was breathy. "We've only shared a kiss. No harm done."

Damn. There'd been plenty of damage. To his sleep, to his peace of mind. Lately, to his sanity.

There was a knock on the door at the bottom of the stairs and Millie called up to her. "Jenny, there's a phone call for you."

"Can you take a name and a message?"

"He says it's important, a Todd Newsome."

Evan watched the blood drain from Jenny's face. "I've got to go."

He stopped her. "What's wrong?"

"Nothing," she said, pulling away, then she went down the steps.

He followed, but she wasn't going to tell him anything. So, she had a past.

She looked back at him. "It would be better if you concentrate on your daughter, Evan. I'll be leaving in a few months. I'll be going back to my job. This has to be the end of it."

Before he could say anything, she took off down the stairs. By the time he reached her, she'd taken the cordless phone from Millie and gone to a quiet corner. Her rejection should drive him away, but he wasn't ready to give up; something wouldn't let him let go of her.

Jenny had prayed she'd never hear from Todd ever again. Her stepbrother had caused her enough trouble to last a lifetime. But over the years he kept showing up like a bad penny.

She punched in the hold button. "What do you want, Todd?"

"Is that any way to greet your big brother, sis?"

"You're not my brother. And I thought you were in jail."

"I got out early for good behavior."

"Fine. Have a good life and stop bothering me."

"Whoa, sis. It wouldn't be a good idea to hang up on me. What would Mom say?"

Jenny stiffened. Her mother had been Todd's only supporter after his last drug offence.

"Go call her and ask." She turned around and saw that Evan was still there. "Look, Todd, I need to go back to work."

"I'd like to do the same, but I don't have a job.

Maybe you can set me up in a job with your fancy friends?"

How did he know? Her mother. She'd probably mentioned her job with the Casalis in letters. "I wouldn't ask any of my friends to hire you. You're unreliable. Shouldn't your parole officer help you find something?"

"I don't particularly want to be a dishwasher or a janitor."

"Why not? It's honest work."

"I think you can do better for me."

"No. I told you years ago, I want you to leave me alone." She felt the familiar panic as she recalled high school and Todd and his creepy friends. That had been the main reason she'd told the police on him. It had gotten him his stay in juvenile hall.

"That's too bad, sis," he told her in a voice that made her shiver. "You owe me, and you're my best bet these days. What's the big deal about helping out a family member?"

"You're not my family. So stay away from me, Todd. I won't help you." Her hands were shaking as she ended the call. No, she wouldn't let him get to her again. The three Newsome brothers had been trouble since day one, but Todd was the worst. She hadn't been surprised that he'd gone to prison.

She turned around and saw Evan watching her. She put on a smile as he walked to her.

"Is everything okay?"

"Of course," she said just as the bell over the shop door chimed and Gracie and Cherry returned, followed by Allison.

"Daddy." Gracie ran to her father. "We need to go home because I have to find some material for the class."

"You have a week before the next class."

The girls didn't like to wait for anything.

"But all the other girls have their moms to help them pick out their material. And grandpa's fixing spaghetti and he said we need to bring Jenny and some bread home. Please, Daddy."

He turned to Jenny. "Looks as if we're outnumbered. Would you like to come to dinner at the Rafferty house?"

It wasn't a good idea. She looked at Gracie and began to lose her resolve. The little girl would be disappointed if she didn't go. "Sure, I'd love to."

CHAPTER EIGHT

An hour later Jenny was seated beside Evan in his truck and on the way to the Rafferty home. How had she got herself into this? Okay, she was a coward. She wanted to be away from any more calls from Todd. No more abuse from her evil stepbrother.

Those days were over.

Thanks to her mother she now had to deal with him again. No doubt Marsha thought Todd had turned over a new leaf, but Jenny doubted he could do anything good, ever.

Time served or not, Todd Newsome was a convicted felon. The last thing she wanted him to do was cause any trouble for her or her friends. She only hoped she'd convinced Todd that she didn't want any more to do with him. Good luck with that. He hadn't cared about her wishes, ever. She couldn't have been happier when he was sent away.

"Jenny," Gracie called.

She turned to the girl in the back seat. "What, sweetie?"

"All the other girls think I'm lucky because I get to take you to my house."

She was touched. "Well, you need help with the project, too. And remember, you have to sew new blocks together."

Gracie nodded. "Daddy, can I have one of your shirts? The one Mommy liked."

Evan frowned. Meg had liked one of his shirts? She'd never said anything to him. "Sure. You'll have to remind me which one that is."

He stole a sideways glance at Jenny, seeing her curious look.

"It's the one you wore when we all went to church on Easter that last time," his daughter said. "I want to use something that Mommy liked."

"Okay, we'll find it then," he said hearing the sadness in his child's voice.

He glanced at Jenny. "Once an altar boy, but I'm not much on church these days."

"Grandpa Sean is Catholic and Mommy and me are Lutherans," the tiny voice came from the back. "What are you, Jenny?"

She smiled. "Oh, I'd say I'm a mixture of a little Catholic with some Presbyterian thrown in. All religions work if you pray."

"At my church they say you have to repent if you do bad things. What does *repent* mean?"

Gracie was too young to hear those kinds of words. "It means to make up for what you did wrong," Evan said. "If you were bad, you should say you're sorry, and then take your punishment."

"Oh. What if that person was really, really mean to me? Do I still have to say I'm sorry?"

Evan stepped in. "If you said something bad to that person, you should."

"But Aaron Jacobs is mean to everybody. He made Sara Hartley cry."

Evan didn't like to hear of someone bullying his child. "Did you tell the teacher?"

He glanced in the rearview mirror and saw her nod.

"But he won't stop being mean to us girls."

"Then I need to have a talk with his parents."

"You will?"

He drove under the ranch archway. "Of course, Gracie. You should have told me sooner."

He pulled up in front of the house. He climbed out and opened the back door as his daughter unfastened her seatbelt and climbed down. Evan squatted down to her level. "Gracie, you can always come to me if you have trouble with any-thing. I'll always be there for you."

She glanced away.

"What's wrong?"

"Mommy always said not to bother you if you're busy 'cause you have a lot on your mind."

He worked to keep his anger under control. "Remember this, Gracie Anne Rafferty. I'm never too busy for you."

A bright smile appeared on her face. "Okay, Daddy."

"Now, go take the bread to Grandpa."

His daughter took the long sticks of sourdough and headed up the steps. Sadness washed over him. Had he been that distant from his own family? Or had Meg deliberately kept him from having a relationship with his daughter? He knew they hadn't had the best marriage, but why had she prevented him from being Gracie's father? If she had, he'd let her.

"Evan, are you okay?" Jenny asked.

"No. My own daughter is afraid to come to me."

"A lot of children go to their mother first."

"Did you?" Suddenly, he remembered Jenny saying her mother was too busy for her. "Or did you have to fight your own battles? How did you handle bullies?"

She shrugged. "I guess I did a lot of my own fighting."

"What about your dad?"

She glanced away. "He was never in my life."

His gut tightened as she tried to seem nonchalant, but he knew it mattered to her. "Well, I'm not going to let Aaron the bully get any more out of control. He has no right picking on little girls." His fists clenched. "I plan to have a talk with this kid."

"Whoa, Rafferty. As a teacher myself, I can tell you it isn't wise to go running off half-cocked. Talk to Gracie's teacher first. Better yet, to Lily Perry. She'll look into the situation, then, if that doesn't help, set up a meeting with the boy's parents."

Evan realized how new this was to him. Had Meg handled this before? Now it was his chance. "Thanks, Jenny."

She nodded. "It's not easy to be a single parent."

"Meg probably would have handled this on her own, too, and never said a word to me." His gaze locked on hers. "Now you know just how perfect my marriage was."

"I'm sorry, Evan." She gave him a sad smile. "But now's your chance to play hero for Gracie."

He frowned. "Whoa, I'm nobody's hero."

"You're going to bat for your daughter. Any girl would love it."

He studied her for a moment. "Who was your hero, Jenny?"

"Not all girls are lucky enough to have one."

* * *

Evan couldn't take his eyes off her. He was getting in deeper and deeper as he watched Jenny. She got along with everyone. Not that Sean and Matt Rafferty weren't pushovers for a pretty woman, but he could see they truly liked her. And Gracie was excited just to have her here. He couldn't remember this much joy during a meal with Meg. In fact, they hadn't had many family dinners. Why hadn't he seen it before? Was he so busy that he didn't take the time to notice? Or had Meg wanted it that way?

Throughout their marriage, it had been that way with most things. Even though he'd put his blood and sweat into this land, for a long time he'd felt more like the Kercher family's hired hand than their son-in-law. Not that he wanted a free pass, but acceptance would have been nice. After their deaths, he and Meg had worked doubly hard to keep striving toward their dream. For the life of him, he couldn't remember now what that was.

Suddenly, laughter broke out, bringing him back to the present as he caught the girls with their heads together, sharing secrets. Gracie looked at him. "Do you know any jokes, Daddy?"

He stole a glance at his dad, then back at his daughter. "I haven't heard a good one in a long time. You tell me one first."

She looked unsure at first, then asked, "Where do snowmen keep their money?"

"I don't know. Where?"

"In a snow bank."

A cute blush covered Gracie's cheeks.

Evan laughed. "Okay, I got one. How do you make a hot dog stand? Steal its chair."

Gracie groaned along with Jenny.

"I know another one. What is a tree's favorite drink? Root beer."

Gracie's eyes widened. "Okay, I have one. Why did the tomato turn red? It saw the salad dressing. Get it? The salad was getting dressed."

Evan loved her responding to him. "What has a lot of keys but can't open any doors?"

"A piano," everyone answered in unison.

"Okay, I guess that one's been around a while."

"It's still funny, Daddy," Gracie assured him. "That was fun. Maybe we can play more games."

Another shock to him. "Okay." Evan stood and began to stack the plates. "Why don't we do the dishes first?"

Jenny got up too. "I'll help."

"Me, too." Gracie picked up her plate and followed everyone to the kitchen.

Jenny enjoyed watching the interaction between Evan and Gracie. She wanted to leave the twosome alone, but it might be too obvious. She returned to the table to clear the rest of the dishes. Sean was there.

"Hey, the cook doesn't clean up," she told him.

"I'll stop after I take these in."

Jenny glanced into the kitchen and saw Evan tie an apron around Gracie's small frame.

"It does my heart good to see those two together." Sean looked at her. "You brought this on, Jenny girl. Sometimes my son has trouble seeing what's right in front of him."

"It would have happened sooner or later," she assured him. "Just the fact that he wants to play an active role in her life means a lot."

Sean sighed. "It should have happened a long time ago. It's sad that Megan and Evan didn't have a better marriage. It was never a perfect match." He beamed. "Except they made the perfect little angel."

Jenny had suspected that things between husband and wife hadn't been as perfect as people believed. "Gracie's precious, and she loves her daddy."

"And my son loves her right back, though he may have trouble showing it." Sean sighed. "Years ago, when his mother left, Evan took it hard. Probably the reason he holds back his feelings."

"We're all afraid of getting hurt," Jenny said,

not realizing she'd said it out loud. "I'd say Evan's pretty lucky to have you and Gracie."

Those big burly arms went around her. "You have us, too, lass. And any father would be blessed to call you his daughter."

She felt tears welling and pulled back. "Thank you. Well, we'd better get these dishes finished so we can play a game before Gracie goes to bed. And I need to get home."

And away from what she'd always wanted. The perfect family.

Two hours later, Jenny closed her eyes in the passenger seat. She was enjoying the quiet music playing on the radio and Evan's company as he drove her back to town.

Talking would only interrupt the intimacy created in the darkness of the truck cab. She was surprised when he reached across the seat and took her hand.

"I have to say, I haven't had such a nice evening in a long time. And Gracie…" He shook his head. "Let's say I haven't seen her this happy since… well, in a long time."

"She's happy because she has your attention."

He pulled into the alley and parked behind the store. There was a soft light overhead, leaving shadows in the cab. He shut off the engine and turned toward her.

"What about you, Jenny? Could you use some attention?" Time slowed as he tugged her gently toward him. He slid his hand around the back of her neck. "I know I'd want some of yours."

She weakly tried to pulled back. "I thought we weren't going to do this?"

"I can't seem to help myself."

Jenny couldn't seem to fight it any longer as Evan leaned down and covered her mouth with his. She was unable to resist his taste and the feel of him. Then she opened her mouth, their tongues touched and there wasn't any denying the desire.

He slipped his fingers into her hair and held her as he explored her mouth. Jenny's hands found his shirt, holding on tight, trying to resist, but she was losing the battle quickly.

This was not a good idea. There were too many reasons to stop, but she couldn't deny what they both wanted. And darn if he wasn't a great kisser.

With the last of her common sense urging her, she pulled back. "Rafferty, we need to stop. This isn't a good idea."

"That's the last thing I want right now. I want you, Jenny Collins."

She pressed her forehead against his. "Don't say that. You need to go home, be with Gracie."

Working to steady his breathing, Evan concentrated on slowing down. He'd never ached for a woman like this, and the last thing he wanted was to leave Jenny tonight.

"My daughter's asleep. This is adult time." He took teasing bites along her jaw, then finally closed his mouth over hers again. It wasn't enough as he tried to pull her closer, moving his hands over her.

Jenny gasped as he worked his hand under her shirt and finally touched her breasts. He wanted more.

He groaned. "You're killing me, woman."

"You started this, Rafferty."

Evan pulled away, looked down at her. He started to speak when something distracted him, and he glanced over her shoulder.

"Someone's in the shop," he whispered and waited. "I see a light moving past the window. And the back door is partly open." He climbed out of the truck and whispered through the open window. "Call the sheriff."

"No!" She grabbed at him. "Evan, you can't go in there."

"Call them." He disappeared through the back door.

Jenny grabbed her cell phone from her purse and punched in the numbers as Evan went inside.

"Emergency, 911."

"Someone broke into the Blind Stitch quilt shop on Main Street," Jenny told the dispatcher. "Please, send someone quick."

"Are you inside, ma'am?"

"No, in the alley behind the store, but my friend went inside."

"Then you stay where you are. A patrol car has been dispatched to the location, so wait for the officer, ma'am."

Jenny was about to hang up when she saw the door open and a shadow appeared. Someone dressed in black took off down the alley. "A man came out of the shop," she said over the phone. "He's running down the alley toward Maple Avenue."

"Okay, ma'am. I'll alert the officer."

She looked back at the doorway, hoping to see Evan come out. He didn't. Oh, no, was he hurt? She dropped the phone, got out of the truck and hurried inside. "Evan!" she yelled. Oh, God, please, let him be okay.

She heard a groan and then a curse. She reached for the shop lights and turned them on. "Evan? Where are you?"

"Here," he said as he appeared from behind the counter.

The sound of sirens pierced the silence. "Oh, Evan, what happened? Are you hurt?"

She reached him, helping him into a nearby chair.

"Not sure," he admitted. "He hit me with something hard." He cursed again. "My head hurts like the devil. I can't believe I walked into that."

She stood back. "Dammit, Rafferty. You shouldn't have gone in at all." She felt the tears well in her eyes. "You could have been really hurt, or worse…" She turned away, unable to say any more.

"Jenny," he whispered her name, reaching for her.

She raised her hand. "Please don't say anything more. I'm barely holding it together."

"Police!" Someone called from the alley, then she recognized Chuck Reynolds, the duty sheriff, as he walked in with his gun drawn. When he saw them, he lowered his weapon. "Evan. Jenny. Are you two okay?"

"No," she told him. "Evan's hurt. Call the paramedics."

"No, don't." Evan reached out and grasped her arm. "I'm fine." He rubbed the back of his head and winced. "We need to talk to Chuck."

Jenny couldn't stop shaking. She'd never been so scared in her life. Another officer moved through the shop into the classroom section. Jenny looked around and did her own inspection. All in all, the shop wasn't in bad shape. The cash register was open, but it had been emptied at closing time. Millie had taken the day's receipts to the bank earlier.

One of the officers came into the room. "The perpetrator ransacked the upstairs apartment."

Jenny's heart sank. She walked toward the back and found Evan on her heels.

"Jenny, wait. You don't need to go up there right now."

"Yes, I do. Everything I own is up there. It's not much, but it's mine."

Evan's head was pounding, but he saw more pain in Jenny's eyes. "Okay, I'll go with you."

"I need to go, too," the deputy said, "and get a list of anything that's missing."

Jenny nodded and the men escorted her up the back staircase to the attic apartment. Evan watched her swallow a sob as she surveyed the mess. Dishes were broken, cushions tossed, furniture toppled over. She walked to the bedroom and saw that the bed had been pulled apart, sheets stripped off, clothes from the closet and dresser thrown on the floor.

"How long were you gone from the shop?"

She looked back at Evan. "Maybe three hours. I was out at the Rafferty ranch."

Evan saw Chuck glance at him, then write down

something. He'd known Chuck in school, and his wife, Claire, had been friends with Meg. Did he care if anyone knew he spent time with Jenny? No.

Chuck ran his hand over his thinning sandy-colored hair. "This could be the work of someone needing drug money. Although robberies are still rare in this community."

Jenny went to the golden-hued brocade-covered box she'd had since childhood. The treasure box was on the floor with its lid torn off. "He took my necklace. Allison and Alex gave it to me for my birthday. There was a small sapphire in the center of a heart." Another tear fell. "It was my birthstone."

"Anything else missing?"

"A few other pieces of jewelry," And, as she checked the dresser drawer, she added, "And about three hundred dollars in cash." She picked up a ragged-looking stuffed bear and hugged it to her body. "Who would do this?"

She paused as if something had come to mind. Her gaze connected with Evan's, then just as quickly she glanced away. "I need to let Allison know what happened." She wiped away the tears and pushed past him out of the room.

Evan looked at Chuck. "What does your gut tell you about this?"

The deputy shrugged. "I don't know. Someone needed money pretty badly." He glanced around the room. "It's odd that the thief bypassed the shop and did all the destruction up here. It seems personal." He looked at Evan. "Does Jenny have any enemies?"

CHAPTER NINE

Two hours later, Jenny sat in the waiting room at the urgent-care facility after she'd finally managed to get Evan checked out. She glanced at her watch. It was after eleven o'clock, she was exhausted and still shaken from what had happened tonight.

What worried her the most was that Todd could have been the one who broke into the shop. Was it possible? Would his parole officer let him leave San Antonio?

Of course, her stepbrother already knew where she was living when he'd called her. And she'd refused to help him. In the past, Todd had never liked it when she didn't do what he wanted. She closed her eyes, trying to fight off the bad memories. Whenever Todd wanted something he'd found a way to get it. He'd been a bully and a trouble-maker all his life. He picked on her because she had told on him many times.

One particular incident when she'd told on him had sent him to juvenile hall. She'd stayed clear of him ever since. Once away at college, she'd heard that he'd been arrested again and this time he was sent to prison.

She had finally felt safe. Until now. She seriously doubted he'd been reformed during his years of incarceration. She knew deep down that he'd had something to do with the break-in. And, if it had been Todd, she couldn't stay here. She couldn't cause her friends any more trouble.

"Jenny Collins."

She looked up to see a nurse, stood and went to her. "Is Evan okay?"

"The doctor will give you the information." She led Jenny back to a curtained cubicle where Evan—minus his shirt—sat on the exam table.

Oh, boy! Her breath caught as she tried not to stare, but she lost the battle. He had a well-developed chest and broad shoulders. His arms weren't bad, either.

He smiled at her. "Doc says I'm lucky he hit me on the head. So it looks like I'm going to live."

"I'm sure your family will be happy to hear that."

An older man with gray thinning hair and a ruddy complexion walked in. "Hello, I'm Charlie Michaels. Everyone calls me Doc Charlie. I've been looking after this guy and his brother most of their lives. By the looks of it, they still can't stay out of trouble."

"I'm Jenny Collins, nice to meet you, doctor. I manage the quilt shop where Evan got injured. This was my fault."

"Jenny, you had nothing to do with the break-in," Evan said. "I'm just glad you weren't there alone."

"Well, you didn't need to rush in and play hero, either," she argued.

The doctor smiled. "I like this one," he said to Evan. "She can hold her own with you."

Evan looked irritated. "Can I go now?"

"Sure. Just remember you have a slight concussion, so don't take anything stronger than ibuprofen. And take tomorrow off work."

"Yeah, right."

"Do you have someone to drive you home and check you during the night?"

"Yes, he does," Jenny said. "Me."

The doctor grinned. "You are a lucky man, Evan Rafferty. And since you're in good hands, I'll go check on patients who really need me." He turned and left them.

"Let's get out of here." Evan stood and slipped into his shirt. It had been one hell of a night. He might have the mother of all headaches, but he was grateful that Jenny hadn't been hurt. He didn't want to think about what might have happened if she'd been there alone at the shop. If this guy was still around, he wasn't letting her out of his sight. Not until he could guarantee she'd be safe.

"Evan, I didn't mean to say I'd be there during the night. Of course I'll drive you back to the ranch, and your dad can check on you. I'll just need your truck to get back to town."

He began tucking his shirttail into his jeans. He caught her watching him and found he liked distracting her.

"You can't stay in your apartment tonight. For one thing it isn't safe, and besides the sheriff is still investigating the break-in."

He went to her and gripped her by the arms. "Jenny, that guy who hit me tonight wasn't messing around. He could be some crazy druggie. You're coming to stay at the ranch."

She glanced away. "I'll go to Allison."

He shook his head. "I already called Dad earlier and told him what happened. He knows you're coming home with me. In fact, he has a room ready for you. And you won't even have to share it with six little girls."

He'd discovered he'd liked having her in his house. So did Gracie and his dad and brother. He had feelings for Jenny, but he still wasn't sure if he was ready to try another relationship.

"Come on, let's go."

He didn't give her a chance to argue as he took her by the arm and they walked out of the exam room. Evan stopped by the desk and signed all the insurance forms, then they headed toward the lobby. He was going to keep her close to him so he could protect her.

Unable to go to her apartment because it was a crime scene, they made a quick stop by the twenty-four-hour drug store. Jenny grabbed some personal items, then they were on their way.

Evan insisted he was okay to drive, so she called Allison and let her know where she'd be. Her friend told her that Alex was out of town, but assured her that the apartment would be cleaned up and new locks installed as soon as the sheriff okayed it. She also offered her a place to stay.

"Thanks, Allison, but I'm acting as nurse for Evan tonight." She couldn't believe she'd said that. "I mean he has a concussion and needs to be watched."

She heard the smile in her friend's voice. "Well, don't let me keep you. I'll talk to you in the morning and the shop will be closed for the day. So don't think about work tomorrow."

"I need to help clean up."

"No, we'll have someone take care of it," Allison told her. "If you're both up to it, come by for supper tomorrow night. Alex will be home and he wants to discuss more security. And bring Gracie."

"Thank you. I'll see how Evan's feeling." Jenny wanted to get off the phone.

"Take care of yourself and Rafferty."

"I will." She said goodbye and closed her phone. "Alex and Allison are going to handle things at the shop. They asked to talk to us so we're invited for supper tomorrow. Gracie, too."

He nodded. "Okay. They're trying to make it easier for you," Evan said, heading out of town. "None of this was your fault."

She wasn't so sure. Again she thought, if this had anything to do with Todd then it was her fault.

Twenty minutes later Evan pulled up to the back of the house. They walked up the steps to the kitchen door, went inside and were met by Sean. He examined his son with a worried gaze, then pulled him into a big bear hug.

"Okay, Dad, you can let go now."

Jenny was next. "Ah, lass. Praise be, you're safe." He pulled her close and she reveled in the warmth of his embrace. She'd never had a father figure growing up. She liked the feeling.

"It's Evan you should worry about. You should also talk to your son about running off to catch bad guys."

Sean shook his head. "Ah, would do little good, the Raffertys are a stubborn bunch. We think we can take on the world." He grinned. "Now, son, go take this young lady upstairs and get her settled in. I'll be down here if anyone needs anything." He kissed Jenny's cheek, then disappeared into the room off the kitchen.

"Tired?" Evan asked her.

She nodded. "Exhausted, but I'm still keyed up."

"Come on, you need to try and get some sleep."

He took her hand and they walked up the stairs. It seemed a natural thing to do, as though they were a couple retiring for the night.

She shook away the crazy thought. At the top of the stairs, he directed her toward a small room. It was a combination office and guest room with a sofa bed pulled out and made up.

"If you're not comfortable here, you can have my room since I'm not going to be sleeping much."

She frowned. "No! I can't sleep in your bed. I mean, I can't take it from you." She motioned to the double-sized sofa bed. "You can't fit in this."

Still holding her hand, he tugged her to him. "I'd definitely make the effort…if you were there."

His head dipped and he covered her mouth with his. She tried to resist him, but found she didn't want to. It felt good to be here, almost too good. Jenny's arms went around his neck as he opened his mouth over hers. With a groan he drew her against him, and she could feel what she was doing to him.

He finally pulled back. "You're killing me, Jenny."

She continued to take soft nibbles from his lower lip, finding it more and more difficult to resist him. "You started it, Rafferty."

"And you're taking advantage of an injured man."

She pulled back. "Oh, I forgot. Are you hurting?"

He gave her a lopsided grin. "That all depends what part of my anatomy we're talking about."

She tried not to smile but lost. "You need to be in bed." She pointed toward the door. "Out. Go and rest in your room."

"Are you sure?"

In the past, she'd always jumped into relationships too fast. And where had it gotten her? And even teasing with Evan didn't mean that he wanted any more.

"Yes. You need to rest. And I need something to sleep in. Do you have an extra pair of pajamas?"

He folded his arms over his chest. "Not since I was eight years old. Would a T-shirt work?"

She nodded, realizing she was fantasizing too much on what he wore. Or didn't wear.

He walked out and returned with a white T-shirt and a soft denim shirt. "A nightshirt and robe. It's the best I can do."

"It's great. Thanks." He started to leave, then he paused at the door and said, "Boxer briefs."

She blinked. "Excuse me."

"Since I have a daughter, I wear boxer briefs to sleep in." He smiled again. "I wouldn't want you to lie awake wondering."

She hated that he could read her. "Thanks, Rafferty, that's kind of you." She held up his T-shirt. "And now you won't have to wonder about what I sleep in." She shut the door chuckling at his groan.

The next morning the sun was barely up when Jenny decided she couldn't stay in bed any longer. She glanced at her cell phone clock and saw it was five-thirty.

She stretched. She hadn't slept much during the last six hours. After she'd checked on Evan at two, he'd informed her he was going to sleep and she'd better too, or he'd find another activity to fill their time.

As much as she wanted the man, she wasn't ready for the next step. Okay, she *was* ready, beyond ready for a man like Evan. But...her past failed relationships made her gun-shy. And now, she had the added complications of Todd and the break-in.

And Evan had his vineyard and was trying to be a parent to his daughter. She had her teaching career back in San Antonio. So many cons to deal with, but she could only think how hard the father and daughter would be to walk away from.

She got up and retrieved her hand washed underwear from the bathroom. She'd showered before bed, so she quickly dressed and went downstairs to see if she could help with breakfast.

Halfway down the staircase she smelled bacon and knew she was too late. There were murmured voices coming from the kitchen and she wondered if she should go back to her room. She spotted Sean about the same time he saw her.

He grinned. "Good morning, lass." He came around the counter and greeted her with a hug.

"Morning, Sean. I came down to help you." She glanced around to see bacon, sausage and pancakes on the table.

"Hello, Matt," she said to the younger Rafferty.

"Morning, Jenny." He smiled. "Now, this is how to brighten the day."

"Stop it, bro," Evan said as he came through the back door. "She's wise to your flirting."

Evan walked up to her and she thought for a minute that he was going to kiss her. He stopped short, but his deep-blue eyes told her he was thinking about it. "How did you sleep?"

"Good." She glanced over him. "How do you feel?"

"Fine. My headache's gone."

"It'd better be," Matt said, then turned to her. "He's helping me brand and inoculate the herd today."

"How many head do you have to do?" she asked.

"It's only about sixty."

"Could you use another pair of hands?"

Both Raffertys stared at her. "You're kidding, right?" Matt said.

"No, I had to help out on my stepfather's ranch. It didn't matter if you were a girl or not." She didn't want to think about those days. "I can't go into work today so you might as well use me here. I'll just need a pair of gloves and a hat."

Matt dropped to one knee. "Oh, Jenny, lass, say you'll marry me," he said in his best Irish accent.

She laughed. "I'll think about it." She glanced at Evan, but he didn't look happy.

"Could this wait until after breakfast?" Sean called. "The food is getting cold."

Evan stood back as his brother found Jenny a seat at the table, as if she couldn't find a place on her own. He even pulled out her chair. That was over the top even for Matt.

"Stop messing around so we can get going."
Evan sat down on the other side of Jenny. Were
they back in high school?

He turned and saw his daughter standing in the
doorway, rubbing her eyes.

"Hey, what's going on?" she said, then spotted their guest. "Jenny!" She rushed to the table.
"What are you doing here?"

"Well, I spent the night in your extra room.
Seems my apartment got messed up yesterday."
She glanced at Evan as if not sure how much to
tell his daughter.

"Gracie, someone broke into the shop last
night. So we didn't want Jenny staying there, and
I brought her home," Evan said.

The child hugged her. "I'm glad. Can you stay
a long time?"

Jenny smiled. "Just today, sweetie. The shop is
closed for only one day, so I'm going to help your
dad and uncle Matt with the branding."

The girl turned to her dad and asked shyly, "Can
I stay home from school and help, too?"

Evan hated this part. "Sorry, honey, not this
time. But if you get all your homework done after
school, we all can go to the Casalis' tonight."

Gracie's eyes lit up and she wrapped her arms
around his neck. "I will, I promise. Thanks,
Daddy."

He swallowed hard. His daughter hadn't asked for much. He'd almost weakened and told her they'd all spend the day together, then Jenny spoke up. "I'll help you."

With a smile that couldn't get any bigger, Gracie went to her seat next to her grandfather. "Grandpa, can I have a pancake, please?"

"You sure can, little one."

Sean went to get a glass of juice and came back with a plate for his granddaughter.

Evan's chest tightened at seeing his child so happy. He wanted to savor every moment of it. He'd missed so much, but he realized he'd let it happen. He hadn't wanted to cause a rift in the efficient home life Meg had made for them. But, in the meantime, he'd been pushed out of so much. No more. He would win his daughter's heart.

He turned to Jenny. Maybe then he could think about rebuilding his own life.

An hour later, Jenny found herself walking with Evan and Gracie to the end of the road where the bus would take her to school.

"You promise you'll be here when I get home?"

"I promise. I'll meet you right here at three-thirty."

With a hug from both her dad and Jenny, Gracie

stepped on the bus and they waited until it drove off and disappeared from view.

Then, suddenly, Evan turned her around and captured her mouth in a sweet and tender kiss, leaving her a little light-headed.

"That's the way I wanted to greet you this morning." He brushed his lips over hers again and again. "But I didn't particularly want an audience."

"And I appreciate that." Still holding his hand, she tugged him toward the house. "We need get back and start work."

He stopped. "Are you that eager, or is it me you're trying to avoid?"

"It's not you, Rafferty. But we need to slow things down a little."

His boots crunched on the gravel road as they walked back. "Isn't that a speech a man usually gives a woman?"

"I'm trying to keep things in perspective. I'll be leaving in a few months. And you have a life here."

"Is that definite?"

She nodded. She was afraid to let herself hope that something permanent would keep her here. The last thing she wanted was to be a replacement wife or mother. She wanted to be the woman that a man couldn't live without. That he'd give up everything for. She shook her head. "I have a responsibility to the kids."

Evan didn't say any more as they passed the foreman's cottage where Matt lived, then headed to the barn where they found his brother.

"Here's the hat and gloves you wanted."

She took the straw Stetson, pulled her hair behind her ears, stuck the hat on her head, then slipped on the gloves. "Pretty good fit."

"I'm a good judge," Matt teased, then sobered. He had the horses saddled and tied to the corral rail. "Okay, you ready to ride?"

"Just tell me which mount is mine."

"Molly," Evan said, stepping in. "She's gentle enough for Gracie, but good at her job."

Matt swung up into the saddle. "Okay, let's get going."

Jenny was suddenly excited. She hadn't done this in a long time. She reached for Molly's reins, put her foot in the stirrup and swung her leg over the mare's back.

Evan showed up beside her. "How's the length of the stirrup?"

"It's fine." She looked at Matt. "You did a good job of judging."

Matt winked. "Told you, I know my women." With that said, he tugged on his reins and rode off.

Evan mounted his gelding, then leaned toward

her. In a swift movement, he leaned forward, cupped the back of her neck and kissed her.

Desire shot through her as his mouth worked over hers. She knew he was staking his claim, but at this point she didn't care. There were times when a woman loved a man taking charge. The right man, that is. He finally released her, and she gasped for air.

"We'll discuss later whose woman you are. Come on, let's go round up some cattle."

CHAPTER TEN

IT took nearly three hours, but they'd managed to round up the herd, separate the mamas from the calves and get them into two pens beside the corral.

Jenny climbed down from her horse, feeling every muscle in her bottom and legs tightening up. Outside of an occasional easy ride, it had been years since she'd spent so much time in the saddle. Today was the real thing, and that included the dust that covered her from head to toe. But at least she hadn't embarrassed herself, and she'd got the job done.

She glanced toward the corral. The young bovines were lined up in a holding area, and Matt was sending them through a cattle chute to be inoculated. The line moved pretty quickly with the three of them working together. She felt the sweat running between her shoulder blades and down her back, but the physical exercise kept her mind focused away from her troubles. The break-in.

They had just finished the last of the cows when a truck pulled up next to the corral. Allison climbed out of the cab.

Jenny walked over. "Hey, what are you doing here?"

Allison handed her a tote bag. "I brought you a change of clothes."

"Thanks. I don't know why I didn't think of it last night."

Allison frowned and nodded toward Evan. "Maybe because you had other things on your mind."

They turned to see Evan as he moved in a slow easy gait, as if he had all day. His coffee-colored chaps hugged long, powerful legs. He had broad shoulders covered in a fitted Western shirt tucked into a narrow waist. Matt was right beside him.

Both men looked good, but Jenny felt her mouth go dry and her stomach tighten for only one. Evan.

Allison leaned close and whispered, "And here I was worried about you." She glanced again at the two men. "Looks like you've been in good hands."

"I haven't been in anyone's hands." She groaned. "I mean, I've been working."

Allison gave her a knowing look just as the men arrived.

"Hello, Allison," Evan greeted them.

"I thought you both were supposed to take the day off," she said.

Evan pushed his cowboy hat back off his forehead. "I feel fine. Has the sheriff contacted you with any leads?"

Allison shook her head. "Alex called, but they're still going over the shop and apartment hoping to find some prints. If we're lucky there'll be some news by the end of the day." She frowned. "You sure you should be working?"

Evan nodded. "You should know roundups can't wait. Besides, my brother here will be busy transporting cattle the rest of the week. So we can't delay it." He turned to Matt. "Matt, this is Allison Casali. Allison, my brother Matt."

"It's a pleasure, Mrs. Casali."

"Please, call me Allison," Allison said. "Do you need Jenny, or can I steal her away for a while?"

"I think we can handle things," Evan said.

"Then we'll go up to the house and talk with Sean," suggested Jenny.

"Hey, will you find out when lunch is?" Evan asked, then turned toward Allison and said, "Please, join us?"

"I'd love to." She smiled. "I hear your dad's barbecue sandwich is the best around."

Evan winked at Jenny. "It's pretty tasty."

"Can't wait," Allison said and hurried to keep

up with Jenny's longer legs. "Here I've been worried and you were out with two good-looking Rafferty men."

"I helped them with the roundup. And if you get closer and take a whiff, you'll know I'm not exactly attractive to a man right now."

"Honey, you've already attracted them. Matt is a flirt, but Evan is serious. He hasn't taken his eyes off you."

"I've been around a lot." She didn't want to hope, or let the few kisses they'd shared sway her. "And I'm helping him with his daughter."

"Like Alex helped me with Cherry."

Jenny stopped, knowing her friend had lucked out when her hero came along and saved the day. "Look, Allison. We've discussed this, I'm leaving in a few months."

Her friend brushed her auburn hair away from her face. "I know, and if there's any way I can talk you into staying, let me know. I mean, you're a teacher of sorts at the Blind Stitch. Who else would take on all those kids?"

"I'm an English teacher, not an expert on quilting. Sometimes I feel like a fraud, trying to fake my way through this."

"The important thing is the kids love you. Everyone loves you. You run a profitable shop, manage classes and even find time to sit with the ladies in the Quilters' Corner."

Yeah, she loved it all, but she wasn't with kids all day. "I love all the women at the shop, but I also love teaching school."

"I bet you'd change your mind if a certain man asked you to stay in Kerry Springs."

Jenny already knew that with a little effort she could fall the rest of the way in love with Evan Rafferty. She wasn't sure if he was ready for another commitment, if ever.

"I can't give up everything for another man. Look what happened with Brian."

They stepped up onto the porch. "Can you tell me you were in love with Brian?"

She shook her head. "Maybe Evan's wrong for me too. I'm just not ready to take another chance."

Allison stopped at the door. "Then tell me one thing, could you love this guy?"

"What's not to love?" That's all she would say as she went inside. She wasn't going to continue this discussion. It was useless. She would leave before it was too late.

By four o'clock the branding had been completed. Evan cleaned up while Jenny and Gracie finished homework. Then, an hour later, they all piled into his truck and headed to the Casali home.

Evan found he liked being a family. He glanced in the mirror at his daughter in the back seat. Correction, part of a family. And the more time he spent with Jenny, the more he thought about how well she fit in. But was he willing to try again? To risk his heart again?

Hell, he didn't know. He knew only that he wanted her like he'd never wanted another woman. He'd never felt this way with Megan. Maybe he hadn't tried hard enough to make his marriage work. His wife hadn't exactly wanted him close, though. They might as well have been in separate beds. Over the years of marriage, they hadn't been more than occasional lovers.

"Evan."

He glanced across the cab. "What?"

"Are you all right?" Jenny asked. "I mean we don't have to go tonight if you're not feeling well."

"No, I'm fine. I don't want to stay too late, though, since Gracie has school tomorrow."

"I'm sure Allison will make sure of that too. But Alex probably wants to go over some things about the security at the shop."

Evan nodded. "I wish I could tell him more about the guy."

Jenny was silent as she stared out the window.

"Did you see anything?" he asked her, still wondering why anyone would destroy Jenny's apartment.

"Only that he was wearing black."

Evan turned down the road to the A Bar A. The ranch was named after Alex and his brother, Angelo. He glanced at the miles of grazing land edged by white, split-rail fencing. The compound came into view. A rancher's dream. Two large barns and several out-buildings dotted the landscape. A large corral contained several purebred quarter horses.

He glanced up the rise to the huge house, snowy white with glossy black shutters framing every window. The lawn was pristine and right in the middle of it was a tricked-out swing set with a slide and a playhouse. What every kid wanted. Something he'd never gotten for Gracie.

"Oh, Daddy, look. See the playhouse? Cherry and me played in it when I stayed overnight here."

He felt bad because he'd never realized little girls liked that sort of thing. He pulled up in the drive as the Casalis came out of the house.

Cherry ran down to greet Gracie and with a hug, they took off. Then Allison walked out with two toddlers in hand, one in a blue shirt and the other in pink, a boy and a girl.

Jenny hurried up the steps and knelt down and hugged them both as they chanted, "Enny. Enny."

"Come here you little munchkins." She hugged the two. Then she looked back at him. "Evan, come meet the kids. This is Will and this one is Rose."

"Hi, guys."

The pair continued to hang on to Jenny as they stared up at him.

"Come down here so they won't be afraid of you."

Evan squatted down and managed a smile. He couldn't believe he was nervous over two kids' opinion of him.

"Will and Rose," Jenny began, "This is my friend, Evan. He's Gracie's daddy."

"Acie," Rose said.

"Yes, Gracie. She's my little girl."

He got a toothy grin from the toddler.

"My kids are shy around strangers," Allison said as the two eyed him suspiciously. "Jenny has been around since their birth. They'll warm up to you soon enough."

"I'm not good with babies."

"You seem to have done fine with Gracie," Allison said.

He shrugged. "Meg did most of the raising." He didn't want to talk about this. "Did Alex make it back?"

"Yes, a few hours ago. He's on his way up from the barn." She glanced around, then smiled.

"There he is." She started down the steps with the twins.

"Look, there's Daddy. Let's go get him. Excuse us, we'll be right back." Allison said.

Jenny watched as the babies toddled across the grass, calling, "Daddy, Daddy." Alex knelt down and caught the two as they ran into his arms. He picked them up and swung them around and they squealed in delight.

She felt her heart tighten. She wanted a family like this, too. She glanced at Evan and saw the longing in his eyes, as well. "Alex waited a long time to find a family. When I first met him he was brooding about everything. He might have been wealthy, but he had no one to share it with. It was Cherry who helped change him. You and Gracie can have that, too."

"He's a lucky guy. Sometimes I feel I do everything wrong," he said honestly.

She frowned. "I'd say you're doing a lot right. Just look at Gracie. She's thriving in the quilting class that you bring her to every week. You participate in her life. Don't be so hard on yourself."

Alex, Allison and the twins made their way to the porch. "Hello, Jenny, Evan." The men shook hands. "Welcome to the Casali family dining experience."

"Hello, Alex."

They started up the back steps and into the kitchen. There was a tall gray-haired woman at the stove. She turned and smiled. "You must be Gracie's daddy. I'm Tilda."

"Hello, Tilda, I'm Evan Rafferty."

"Well, welcome. Now let's get the children settled and eat supper." Alex put the kids in their high chairs as Cherry and Gracie walked in.

Once everyone was settled at the kitchen table, and the blessing said, they began to eat the pot-roast dinner Tilda had prepared. Over the next thirty minutes there was chaos and food everywhere.

It was a great time.

An hour later, Gracie was upstairs in Cherry's bedroom watching a video. Allison and Jenny were giving the twins their baths.

Alex led Evan into his office. "As soon as the sheriff finished today, I got a locksmith to change all the shop's locks, including a separate deadbolt that has been installed on the door leading upstairs to Jenny's apartment." He shook his head. "I should have checked the security before she moved in. If I have to, I'll keep a twenty-four-hour guard at the door until we find this guy."

Evan found he wanted to be that guard. Her

protector. But would she allow that? "So there are no leads?"

Alex shook his head. "No fingerprints other than Jenny's. And forget downstairs, there have been too many people in and out of the shop. We have to hope this is a onetime thing."

"Has anyone else in the area been robbed?"

"The sheriff said this was the first. And I hope it's the last."

Allison walked into the room. "I'm exhausted," she said, sitting down in one of the overstuffed chairs. "You have no idea what your kids put me through."

Alex tilted back in his seat. "Now they're mine."

"Okay, I'll make a deal with you. You bath them the next time and you can call them my kids."

Evan enjoyed the easy banter between husband and wife. There was no doubt these two loved each other. He shook his head. "One child is hard enough, but two. It seems impossible."

Allison nodded. "And I'm getting older by the minute."

"I'll do their bath tomorrow night," Alex promised.

"Oh, no, you don't. Last time the three of you caused water damage. It's not worth the cleanup."

Evan stood. "Well, I'll go find the girls and head out." They didn't even notice his leaving. He had started to go hunt for Gracie, when he spotted Jenny standing at the back door talking to someone. He walked closer and discovered it was Brian Perkins.

Great. He walked over. "Jenny, I wondered where you'd gone to." He smiled at her, then forced one for the man. "Hello, Perkins."

"Rafferty. How are you?"

"Not too bad." He slipped an arm over Jenny's shoulders. "Not bad at all."

Brian looked at her, too. "I just came to see if Jenny was okay. If there's anything I can do, let me know."

"Not to worry, I've got it under control."

Brian held his gaze. "Then I'll leave her in your hands. Bye, Jenny."

"Bye, Brian."

They watched him walk away and Jenny turned around and glared at him. "Don't you dare treat me like that again."

"What are you talking about?"

"Don't play innocent with me, Evan Rafferty. You wanted Brian to think something was going on between us."

"So what if I did? What if I want something between us?"

Her brown eyes widened. "It would be nice if you let me know your feelings first." She turned and headed out the door. He had started after her when he saw Gracie standing on the stairs. He could tell by the look on her face that she'd heard everything. Great, that was all he needed.

"Daddy, is Jenny mad at you?"

Don't lie. "Yeah, I did something to upset her."

She stood in front of him. "Then you need to tell her you're sorry."

He put his arm around his daughter and pulled her close. "I plan on it, and a lot more."

By eight o'clock, Evan had everyone back at the house. Jenny helped Gracie with her bath and got her into bed. And she managed to stay clear of the girl's father.

He had to put a stop to that; with a soft knock he walked into his daughter's room. He watched the interaction between Jenny and Gracie with envy. Story ended, she kissed Gracie good night and didn't even look at him.

In the past few weeks, he'd found he and his daughter were easier around each other. The affection between them was more natural. Maybe he really was capable of doing this.

After kissing Gracie, he was almost out the door when she called, "Daddy, don't forget."

"I won't, honey. I promise, it'll be okay."

Once the door was closed, Jenny gave him a questioning look. "What promise?"

"My daughter says I need to apologize to you for earlier."

Jenny waited.

"Okay, I acted like a jerk. I'm sorry. But I only wanted to protect you. Perkins hurt you before."

"I'm a big girl, Rafferty. I can take care of myself."

"What if I want to take care of you?" He took her hand, finding he didn't want her to leave. "You could still stay here and I'll drive you back early in the morning."

"Thank you for the invitation, but I need to face it sooner or later. I need to go back. I can't live in fear all the time."

"Okay, but I'm checking the place out thoroughly before I leave."

"I wouldn't mind that at all. Now take me home, cowboy."

Evan parked in the alley. There were several more lights illuminating the area, along with a security camera over the door.

"Geez, a guy would be crazy to come back here."

"I just hope I can get the alarm shut off after I get inside."

"Let's go try it. You've got the code."

With her nod, they got out and Jenny inserted the new key into the deadbolt lock. She opened the door and saw the panel on the wall, then quickly punched in the numbers and it shut off.

"Okay." She sighed. "That's done." She went to the other new lock on the door leading to her apartment. She opened it, flicked on the light and started up the stairs.

Jenny was pleasantly surprised to see that everything had been cleaned and put away. "This is even nicer than the way I kept it."

Evan knew that Casali could get things done fast, but this surprised even him. There was no sign the place had been trashed.

The sofa had been replaced along with tables and lamps, even a new television. He followed her into the bedroom and found the furniture there was also new.

Jenny turned to see her childhood treasure box on the table. It meant a lot to her. She'd never had much, but this was something from a happier time in her life.

Evan came up behind her. "I'm sorry you lost your personal things."

She shrugged. "They were only things."

His hands rested on her shoulders, his head close to her ear, and he whispered, "I thank God you weren't here alone." His warm breath caused her to shiver. "And you aren't alone now, Jenny. I want to be here for you."

She closed her eyes, aching to lean into this man. Yet, she was afraid.

"I won't let anything happen to you," he promised.

She wanted to believe him. In her lifetime a lot of people had let her down. They had let things happen to her, things a child shouldn't have to go through.

"Tell me what you're feeling, Jenny." He turned her around, his blue eyes steady on hers. "Tell me what I can do to help you."

She allowed him to take her hands and put them behind his neck, just as his head lowered to hers.

Then his hungry mouth claimed hers, taking long deep kisses. She could only cling to him. Her body burned as he stroked her from her waist to her breasts. His hands moved to cover her nipples, which quickly hardened against his palms. She made a whimpering sound at the sheer thrill.

He tore his mouth from hers, his eyes smoldering as he rained kisses over her face. "I want you, Jenny. You have no idea."

"I think I do." She stood up on her toes and pressed her mouth against his. This time she wasn't shy about her hunger as she slipped her tongue against his lips. He opened readily as she slipped inside, drawing a deep groan from Evan. He tightened his hold and returned the favor. She moaned this time.

She was rapidly falling under his spell and was so tired of fighting it. She pulled back slightly. "I want you, too, Evan. Don't leave me."

He cupped her face, then brushed a kiss over her mouth. "I'm here. I'm here for you as long as you want me."

Forever! She longed to say it, but didn't dare. Instead, she kissed him, then kissed him again. She wanted to burrow into him, absorb his warmth and his strength. He seemed to go for the idea, too. His breathing ragged, he held her still.

"I want to make love to you, Jenny. So if it's not what you want, too, I'll sleep on the sofa. But just so you know, I've never felt this way about a woman before. Ever."

Evan Rafferty filled more than the loneliness and made her feel so much more. He made a girl dream of forever.

"I want that, too, Evan. So much."

"I like it when you say my name." His mouth covered hers, refusing to let her say any more.

The next time they broke apart, he took her by the hand and together they walked into the bedroom. She wasn't thinking about anything other than how much she wanted this man.

He turned on the dim bedside lamp, then he came back for her. He slowly began removing her blouse, all the while touching her, caressing her, until she was moaning with need.

She did the same for him. Soon his shirt was gone, and she moved her hands on his heated skin. He was hard and muscular, but his skin was smooth and sensitive to her touch. "You're beautiful."

"I'm glad you think so." He was having difficulty breathing. "You're killing me here."

He finally took back the reins and unhooked her bra clasp. "I believe you're the gorgeous one here." His mouth moved over hers and down her jaw. "I think we should test the new mattress."

He tugged on her hand, and she went willingly as he pulled her across the small room to the bed. In between kisses, he helped her remove her boots and jeans, then he swiftly stripped off the rest of his clothes.

He climbed in beside her, the warmth of his body against hers causing her to sigh. She could stay like this forever.

That was the problem. She didn't have forever.

CHAPTER ELEVEN

JENNY awoke with the rising sun and was surprised to find Evan still here, only not in her bed. She felt her heart tighten as she thought back to last night and how tenderly he'd made love to her. The man spoke few words; instead he'd shown her by his actions how much he wanted her.

Over and over again.

She smiled to herself as she looked toward the doorway. Her lover stood in a pair of jeans and his boots, his shirt opened, exposing his chest. Very sexy.

"Didn't mean to wake you," he told her.

Had he been going to sneak out without saying goodbye? "You didn't, I'm usually up with the sun." Suddenly she was very conscious of her nakedness. "How long have you been awake?"

"Not long." He raised a mug. "I made coffee." He brought it to her.

She held the sheet against her breasts as she sat

up. Suddenly they were like strangers. "Evan, is something wrong?"

He looked away. "I'm not good at this."

She took it he meant the morning after. "Neither am I."

He raised his head, looking concerned. "Do you want me to leave? If you need some privacy…"

She touched his arm. "No, I want you to stay, Evan, but only if you want to."

Evan wasn't sure what he wanted. Last night had changed everything. He couldn't seem to stop his feelings for her. "Hell, Jenny, I'd like nothing more than to continue this, but I need to get home. Gracie won't understand why I'm not there."

She looked disappointed. "You're right. This might be a little hard to explain to an eight-year-old."

Feeling more insecure than ever, Jenny grabbed her robe off the chair at the end of the bed and slipped it on, covering her nakedness. So, she was a woman he couldn't explain?

She stood and walked out of the bedroom. It was glaringly clear that last night meant something different to Evan. She'd hoped for something permanent, but he apparently wanted something casual.

She went to the refrigerator and had taken out a bottle of water when Evan appeared behind her.

"Jenny?"

She couldn't look at him. "What?"

He turned her around to face him. His incredible blue eyes searched her face. "Last night was... special."

"It was for me, too," she said softly.

He pulled her against him and captured her mouth. His heated kiss quickly had her thinking how easy it would be to fall in love with this man. Too late—she was already there.

He broke off the kiss, but held her tight for a moment, then released her. "I've got to go." He stepped back. "I'll call you later."

She nodded, feeling too vulnerable to speak. They went down the stairs, and she let him out the back door, and then reset the alarm system.

She leaned against the door and touched her lips. Did she dare hope that this was the beginning of something? Something permanent?

She'd always been the eternal optimist in the happily-ever-after department. She'd had her heart broken a few times, but, as Allison had told her repeatedly, there was someone out there for her.

Jenny had always thought that women who'd found Mr. Perfect would say something like that. She wanted to believe it. She desperately wanted to believe that Evan Rafferty was her Mr. Perfect.

* * *

Evan walked through the back door at the house to find his family seated at the table eating breakfast.

His dad was the first to speak. "Did you get the waterline in the barn fixed?"

So his dad was giving him an out for his early-morning absence. "Yeah, it's working fine now." Why did he suddenly feel like a teenager again? He went to his daughter and kissed her on the cheek. "Morning, sweetie."

"Morning, Daddy." She rubbed her face. "Your beard is scratchy."

He went to grab a cup of coffee from the counter. "That's because I didn't have time to shower and shave. I promise I will before you come home from school."

His brother finally raised his head from his eating. "Are you up to helping me load the cattle in the trailer?"

Evan nodded. "I told you yesterday I would."

Matt shrugged. "That was before the…waterline broke."

"That shouldn't make any difference, nothing has changed." He turned to his daughter. "Gracie, you'd better hurry up, the bus will be here soon."

She stood. "Okay, I need to get my books. I've got a spelling bee today."

"I'm sorry, I didn't know."

She smiled. "It's okay, Jenny's been helping me."

Why hadn't he known about this? "Well, get out the list anyway and we'll practice on the walk to the bus."

Gracie smiled and took off. He turned to his dad and brother. They both tried to act as if this were a normal morning.

"Okay, say it. Get it off your chests."

His dad shrugged. "What's to say? You're a grown man. Jenny is a wonderful woman." Sean's gaze met his. "Sneaking around isn't a good idea, son. She deserves better."

Matt didn't look too happy, either.

"You might as well give me your opinion, too."

His brother set down his fork. "I see how she looks at you. Man, she's crazy about you. If you're just toying with her, do her a favor and let her go before she gets hurt." He stood and carried his plate to the sink. "I'll be out by the pens." He walked out the door.

"What's his problem? He's with a different woman every weekend, and he's lecturing me."

His father stood. "None of those women are Jenny Collins."

Since the Blind Stitch had been closed yesterday, Jenny had had a busy morning—most of the regular patrons had stopped by to see how everything was going.

Finally grabbing a break, she sat down at the table in the Quilters' Corner. Beth Staley, Liz Parker and Louisa Merrick were now the mainstays at the table. Two young mothers, Lisa and Caitlin, tried to spend as much time there as they could manage. These women had been meeting a few times a week and worked on projects most of the morning. One joint project had been making baby quilts for the hospital fund-raiser.

"Aren't you frightened to stay here alone now?" Beth asked Jenny.

She hadn't been alone yet. "Not really. Allison's husband put in a new security system. And the sheriff is patrolling the area."

Beth shook her head. "I'm a woman without a man, too. I'd hate to think there's someone out there preying on women."

Jenny didn't want to believe the guy was still hanging around. "The sheriff thinks it might be someone who wanted fast money. He didn't get away with much because Millie had already taken the day's receipts to the bank."

"But he was in your apartment," Lisa added. "I hear he made a mess of everything."

"And I have new locks there, too, and I feel safer," she lied. She wanted this guy caught, too. She wanted it to be over, because she knew that Evan couldn't spend the night again.

Millie walked in, carrying the phone. "Call for you, Jenny."

She took the receiver, hoping it might be Evan. "Excuse me." She stood and walked to a quiet corner in the classroom area. "Hello, Jenny Collins."

"Hello to you, too, little sister," her stepbrother said.

She tensed as fear raced through her. "Todd, I told you not to call me again."

His voice had a frightening tone. "Since when do you tell me what to do?"

"Look, I don't want any trouble from you. I just want to be left alone."

"Come on, Jen. We're family. I'm only asking for a little help. If you recommend me for a job with your friend's rich husband, I won't bother you at all."

"I can't, Todd," she insisted. "Now leave me alone."

"That's a shame, sis." There was a long pause. "I hear there was a break-in the other night. They made a mess out of the place."

She froze. How would he know unless he was in town and he... "It *was* you," she hissed.

"Jen, Jen, Jen. There you go accusing me of the worst. Just like when you were a kid."

With good reason, she thought.

"Besides, there's no proof it was me," he told her. "Of course, if I had a job, I'd have an income. Otherwise I could be tempted to revert back to my old ways. And it would be all your fault. Think about it."

"Leave me alone." She hung up, but she couldn't stop shaking. Oh, God. It was Todd. He'd broken into her apartment. He'd touched her things, taken her money.

What could she do? Nothing. Todd was right—she had no proof that he was the one who'd broken in. She did know that her stepbrother was capable of a lot worse than trashing an apartment and a shop. She couldn't let him hurt her friends, people she loved, because she wouldn't give him what he wanted. Now she had no doubt about her decision to leave.

"Jenny, is everything all right?"

She turned around to see Millie's concerned look. She couldn't drag her friends into this mess. "It soon will be."

By midmorning, they'd loaded the rest of the yearlings and latched the gate on the truck. Matt hadn't talked to Evan since breakfast except to shout orders.

Evan had had enough. "Why don't you just say it and get it off your chest?"

His brother gave him a questioning look.

"Don't play dumb, Matt."

"Okay, if you want to hear it. I don't like the way you're treating Jenny. Do you even care about her?"

Why was everyone in his business? "Of course I care."

"If that's true, why haven't you called her? After all, you spent the night with her."

He was planning on calling her later. Maybe taking her to dinner, but his brother didn't need to know that. "This isn't high school."

"Women still want the same things. You need to let her know that she means something to you. Or do I need to pound some sense into you?"

"Whoa, what is this? You go out with different women all the time. Why do I get grief because I spend time with one?"

Matt glared at him. "If I was lucky enough to find someone like Jenny, I wouldn't be out there looking."

Evan knew Jenny was special. She also made him feel things. Things he wasn't sure he wanted to chance feeling again.

His brother wasn't finished. "Okay, I know Megan played a number on you, but Jenny is nothing like her. She's honest and loving. Man, you are one lucky son of a gun."

He thought about last night, about how giving Jenny had been. She wasn't afraid to show him her wants and desires, or to please him. My God. What had he done? "I know that."

"Then do something. Send her flowers, tell her how you feel."

"I'm not sure I'm ready for that."

Matt shook his head. "Okay, you don't need to say the L-word. But let her know you're thinking of her. You *are* thinking about her, right?"

Evan nodded. "Hell, yes. I can't think about anything else."

There was a hint of a smile. "Then call her," Matt insisted. "No, send her flowers *and* say it, too."

Evan pulled out his cell phone. He must really have it bad if he was listening to his brother's advice.

Since Todd's phone call, Jenny had barely made it through the afternoon, then the small bouquet of spring flowers arrived at the shop.

"Oh, my, who are they for?" Millie asked the delivery man.

"Jenny Collins."

Jenny's head jerked up. Who would send her flowers? "Me?" She grabbed some bills out of her wallet to tip the man as he set the vase on the counter.

"Well, open the card," Liz said, as the rest of the ladies hurried toward the counter.

With shaky hands, she opened the card and read it to herself. "Thinking about you. Will you go to dinner with me tonight? Evan."

"Who are they from?" Millie asked.

She felt her chest tighten. "Evan Rafferty." Tucking the small card into her pocket, she rushed on to say, "I've been helping his daughter with her quilting project."

The group smiled, then Louisa said, "He's a nice young man," and everyone wandered back to the corner table. Jenny was near tears. Why did he have to be so nice? Why did she have to fall more and more in love with him? Why now, when she had to give him up? When she had to give up everything that she'd come to care about? Yet it was the only way to guarantee that Todd would stay out of their lives.

She picked up her phone and made a call to the San Antonio high-school district. She'd always planned to leave Kerry Springs, but the reality of it so soon really sucked.

As she hung up, the back door opened and Deputy Reynolds walked into the shop along with Alex. She put on a smile and went to them.

"How did it go last night?" the deputy asked. "Any trouble?"

Jenny glanced away. "It was fine. Everything was fine. I doubt anyone could break in here again." She forced a smile, hoping he couldn't see through her lie.

"I'm glad to hear that," Alex said. "If someone does break in, you know you have a panic button that connects to the sheriff's department?"

She nodded. "The guy's probably long gone."

"But if you don't feel safe here, you can always stay out at the ranch."

She couldn't ask for any better friends than the Casalis. So she couldn't let Todd get too close. "I'll be fine."

"Well, I should go," the deputy said, checking his watch. "I need to alert the next shift to what is going on."

The deputy left but Alex hung back. "Oh, by the way, your stepbrother came by the ranch."

She froze. "What?"

"Todd Newsome came by wanting to sign on for the roundup. He used you for a reference."

She couldn't breathe. Oh, no, it was already happening. She swallowed the dryness in her throat. "He did?" She straightened. "I don't know why he'd use me, we never got along."

Alex studied her for a moment. "That's all I need to know." He walked out the back door.

Okay, now she had no choice. She had to leave. No matter how much she loved it here and loved these people, she couldn't stay. Todd would never leave her alone, not as long as he thought he could have an in with her influential friends. He wouldn't stop short of hurting someone.

She drew a breath and released it. She'd talked to her school principal earlier that day. The semester didn't start until August, nearly three months away, but she'd been able to snag a summer-school job and a substitute position starting next week. The sooner she got out of town the better for everyone—except her.

Evan had tried to phone Jenny all afternoon trying to get an answer, but he kept getting her voice mail. Finally she'd called the house and left a message with his dad saying she couldn't go out with him.

He decided he needed to know what was going on and arrived at the back door at the scheduled time. That was when he saw Jenny throwing boxes into the Dumpster. He parked and got out, calling to her.

She turned around, looking surprised to see

him. "Evan. Didn't you get my message that I couldn't go tonight?"

He was confused. "Didn't you get my flowers?"

She smiled faintly. "Oh, yes, and they were lovely. Thank you." She glanced around nervously. "I need to go back to San Antonio immediately. So I need to pack."

What had changed? "Is there a family emergency?"

"No. I had an opportunity to take a teaching job for the summer."

"I know I left abruptly this morning, but I needed to get home. You understood why, didn't you?"

Her gaze didn't meet his. "Of course I did. Maybe it made me realize that with a child involved, things got moving too fast. I'm just not ready to start up another relationship."

He didn't want to lose her. "Okay, maybe we jumped ahead last night a little fast. We can slow things down."

"It will have to slow way down." She shrugged. "As a rule, long-distance relationships don't work out. I'm sorry, Evan, I know that's not what you want to hear. I told you I had a teaching job."

"Then why race out of here? I thought you weren't returning to San Antonio until fall?"

She refused to meet his gaze. "I have a chance

to substitute-teach for the rest of this semester." She took a breath. "Maybe it's for the best."

She started to walk inside, but before the door closed, he pushed his way in behind her. "Maybe best for you, but not for me. And what about Gracie? Talk to me, Jenny. What's really the reason?"

Her gaze darted away. "There's nothing more to say. You're a wonderful man, Evan. But I was always going to leave. It just happens to be sooner than I thought."

"How soon?"

"A few days."

His heart began to pound hard. "I thought things were changing between us. I guess I was wrong."

Tears filled her eyes. That gave him hope.

"I have kids who are depending on me, Evan. I love teaching school. You knew that."

He wanted to know if she cared about him at all, if he could change her mind. "Would it make any difference if I asked you to stay?"

Even as a tear found its way down her cheek, she quickly shook her head. "Oh, Evan, I can't. It's better this way. I'm sorry."

He got that familiar feeling. He wasn't enough for her, enough for her to stay. Maybe he just wasn't cut out for relationships.

"Nothing to be sorry about. You either feel

something or you don't. At least we discovered it before we got in too deep." He drew her into his arms and held her close. Jenny didn't resist. When he pulled back slightly, all he could see was the woman to whom he'd opened up, the woman who'd given him hope that they could share a future. Looked like he'd been wrong about her.

He lowered his head and touched her mouth with his. He intensified the kiss, wanting to brand her, so she'd remember him. When she whimpered softly, he finally released her. "Have a great life, Jenny. Goodbye."

The evening got even worse when Jenny drove to the A Bar A. Her friend greeted her at the kitchen door. She could still remember the first time she'd met Allison Cole when she'd signed up for her quilting retreat. She'd also got to watch as her friend fell in love with Alex Casali. Yeah, she had envied what Allison had found. So much so she'd tried to find the same thing with Brian. There wasn't any fairy-tale ending for Jenny, not then or now.

They'd all become good friends. She'd had a family unlike anything she'd ever known. Now, she had to give them up, before Todd tarnished that, too. She thought about the Raffertys, knowing she'd lost them already.

She parked and went to the back door and knocked. Allison greeted her with a surprised look on her face.

"Not that I don't like seeing you, but I wasn't expecting you all the way out here tonight. What's so important that it couldn't wait until tomorrow?" she asked.

"I'm going back to San Antonio. A teaching job became available."

Allison studied her. "How soon?"

"In a few days."

Without comment Allison walked down the hall and came back with Alex.

"I hear you're leaving us," he said. "What do I need to do to make you want to stay? If it's money, we can pay you more. You're definitely worth it."

God, this hurt more than she'd ever imagined. "It's not the money, Alex. You both always knew I'd be going back to teaching. I have a chance for placement by substituting for the last few weeks of the semester, then teaching summer school. But I have to start immediately."

He studied her for a moment. "I don't know why, but I have a feeling there's more. But you aren't willing to share that yet." He reached out and gripped her by the arms. "Jenny, if there's ever anything you need, don't hesitate to call us. You are *famiglia. Per sempre.*"

Family forever. She fought to hold it together. "Thank you. I love you both and the kids so much." She couldn't stay. If she did she'd blurt out everything. "After I get settled I'll call and come back for a visit."

"You'd better," Allison threatened. "And we can come and visit you. San Antonio isn't that far way."

Jenny managed a nod. She had to stay away from people she cared about for a while, until Todd found someone else to prey on. She refused to let him hurt the people she loved. People who truly cared about her.

She thought about Evan and Gracie. She'd never recover from losing them.

CHAPTER TWELVE

"JENNY is going away?" Gracie said to her dad when she got off the bus the next afternoon. "Forever?"

Evan was trying to soften the pain. "She's going back to her home in San Antonio."

"But she can't." Panic showed in Gracie's blue eyes. "She's helping me with my part of the quilt."

That was the last thing Evan wanted to think about, but right now his daughter was his number-one priority.

He squatted down, seeing her fight tears. "We'll figure out something, honey. Maybe one of the other ladies can help you."

"I don't want anyone else." She sobbed and collapsed into his open arms. He held her small body against his chest, absorbing her tears. He'd never seen her cry like this. When her mother had died, she'd gone into her bedroom and wouldn't let him in. This was the first time she'd let him get close enough to share her pain, and he couldn't do anything to make her feel better.

"It's going to be okay, sweetie. I'm here. I'll always be here for you."

She drew back and looked at him through watery eyes. "Do you want Jenny to go away?" The child didn't wait for an answer. "I know she wants to be with us. She doesn't have a family who loves her like we do. Who's going to take care of her? She always helps everybody."

Evan remembered Jenny saying her mother never had time for her. And there was that panicked look when her stepbrother had called her. "I wish I could, but she told me she wants to teach her kids. She'll be so happy to be back in her classroom." Did it even matter that they'd all be miserable without her? How could she just walk away from everyone who cared about her?

Silently they made their way back to the house and into the kitchen. His father greeted them. "Hello, Evan, and my little one," he said.

"Hi, Grandpa."

"I have your favorite snack ready."

She glanced at the sliced fruit, cheese and crackers. "No thanks, I think I'll go to my room and do my homework." She walked out looking sad. More sad than Evan had ever seen her.

"I'll be up later to help you," he called to his daughter.

"She didn't take the news well?"

Evan shook his head. "She cried. It breaks my heart."

His dad cocked an eyebrow. "What about your heart, son?"

He was numb. He didn't want to talk feelings. "What difference does it make? Jenny's leaving and I can't stop her."

"Maybe you didn't try hard enough."

"Yes I did. I told her I wanted to build something together. I even pulled out the Gracie card. She never budged."

Sean shook his head. "I don't believe it. I've seen how that girl looks at you. She cares, son. There has to be something else."

"She has a teaching job."

Sean frowned. "Even I don't believe that, son. Jenny's not the kind of girl to get so close to a man, then just walk away. Beside there's teaching jobs here."

Evan's thoughts returned to their night together. The things they'd shared. It couldn't have been only about physical pleasure; there was more between them. And he had to know for sure. "I need to call Allison."

He pulled out his phone and made the call as he walked outside to the porch.

"Casali residence," Alex answered.

"Alex, it's Evan. I need to know the real reason Jenny is leaving."

"Believe me, I've tried everything to get her to stay. Allison and the kids are heartbroken."

He and Gracie weren't much better. "Then we need to figure this out. You have any ideas?"

"My suspicions are that this has to do with her stepbrother," he said. "Todd Newsome came out to the ranch the other day looking to sign up for the roundup. He used Jenny's name as a reference."

That sent up a red flag. "Did you give him a job?"

"No, Jenny did not recommend him when I mentioned it. I had him checked out with the sheriff. He's recently been released from prison."

That explained a lot. "Prison? What was he in for?"

"Drugs," Alex told him, then he went on to say that after five years, he'd got an early release. "He put down a San Antonio address, but then he shows up here."

Evan thought back to the phone call Jenny had received from her stepbrother. "Newsome called her last week. She didn't sound happy to hear from him."

"Damn, why do I have this nagging suspicion he had something to do with the break-in?" Evan heard a sigh. "And you aren't going to like this either. There was another break-in last night. Harley's Pawn Shop."

Evan cursed. "You're thinking Todd could be involved in this?"

"I'm saying it seems strange things started happening when the guy arrived in town. And now Jenny's suddenly leaving town. It has to be because she's protecting us from the SOB," Alex surmised.

It was all making sense now. "Then we need to protect her and set this right," Evan said.

The next afternoon Jenny finally told Millie and the women in the quilters' circle that she was leaving. She'd already packed most of her clothes and personal things. Since her furniture was in storage, there hadn't been much to move.

She didn't even have a place to live in San Antonio. She definitely wasn't going to stay with her mother and stepfather. For her own safety, she had to keep as far away from Todd as possible.

The bell over the door rang and she glanced up to see little Gracie, dressed in a skirt and blouse covered partly by a green sweater, and carrying her backpack. Her dark hair was pulled up in a ponytail and she looked as though she'd lost her best friend.

Jenny felt her heart sink, knowing she had to talk to this child.

She put on a smile and went to her, glancing around for Evan. "Hi, Gracie. Does your daddy know you're here?"

The girl shrugged.

"Sweetie, you know you can't come here if your daddy doesn't know where you are."

"But I have to stop you from going away." Tears sprang to the child's eyes as she rushed on to say, "Please, stay, Jenny. I don't want you to go away."

Jenny's throat tightened, tears filling her own eyes as she knelt down and hugged her. "Oh, Gracie." She loved this little girl and her father so much. "There's nothing I'd like more, but I have a job." Which she'd give up in a second to stay here in Kerry Springs.

Gracie wiped her eyes. "But why can't you stay and marry my daddy and be my mommy?"

Jenny was caught off guard by the innocent question, but her heart filled with love for this child. "Oh, Gracie. That's a wonderful thought, but…" She wasn't sure how to answer her question. Although she wanted nothing more, Evan hadn't asked her.

"If you told Daddy you wanted to be in our

family he'd marry you," Grace insisted. "He was so sad before, and when you're here, he's happy. Please ask him, Jenny. Please."

The girl began to sob and Jenny consoled her. "I'll talk to him, sweetie," she told Gracie. "But no promises." Jenny stood, pulled out her phone and punched in Evan's number. She walked away from Gracie as the familiar voice came on the line.

"Jenny?"

"Evan, I wanted you to know that Gracie is here at the shop. I think she missed the school bus."

He cursed. "Keep her with you, I'm in town already so I'll be there right away."

"Okay," she managed to say and hung up. She had to face Evan one more time, and she hoped she could get through seeing him without breaking down. She was doing the right thing, she'd been telling herself. He wasn't ready for a relationship and she didn't have the option of waiting, giving it a chance to develop into more. Not with Todd's threats. Their one night together had been like a dream. Now, she had to face reality and walk away from everything she'd ever wanted.

She returned to the front of the shop and found someone with Gracie. She studied the familiar-looking man and it hit her—he was thinner but more muscular, and there were tattoos covering his upper arms. His hair was cut shorter, but she'd recognize Todd Newsome anywhere.

She felt her panic building as she watched him talk to the child. It looked innocent enough, but she knew it wasn't. Todd was here to give her a message.

"Gracie, I talked to your dad, and he's coming to get you." She smiled at her. "Now, go wait in the office and you can start your homework."

Todd took a step closer to the girl. "Ah, sis, we were just getting to know each other."

She ignored him. "Gracie, do as I say."

The girl went into the back as Jenny stood facing her stepbrother. "Todd, I told you, I don't want you here."

"That's too bad, Jen. We can't always have what we want. You stopped me from getting a job with Casali. So I had to take things in my own hands."

She refused to back down. "I didn't stop it. They probably checked your record."

"If you had put in a good word for me, Casali would have hired me." He grabbed her by the arm with a tight grip. It hurt, but she wouldn't show it. "It wouldn't have been hard for you. Since you're the one who sent me to Juvenile Hall in the first place, you owed me."

"You trashed my shop and apartment. And I

know you had something to do with the break-in at the pawn shop, didn't you?"

Shaking his head, Todd tossed her a sinister grin. "I warned you about blaming. I remember another time you opened your mouth and got me into trouble with the cops." He stared at her. "I wouldn't try it again, if I were you. If for some reason I get arrested, wouldn't your friends think you might have something to do with it?"

She jerked away. "Why can't you just leave me alone?"

"You owe me, sis. I went to jail because of you."

She got behind the counter. "You went to jail because of what you did."

"And because your mother favored me over you. Poor baby." His grin scared her. "Since you refused to help me, I had to do things on my own. I have a job. A good one."

"Here? You got a job in town?"

"Oh, yes. Kerry Springs is such a nice community and it has interesting possibilities." He grinned at her. "And, of course, you're living here."

"Well, I don't want you in Kerry Springs." She couldn't leave him in town. "Besides I'll be gone soon. Shouldn't you go, too?"

"Why, sis, if I didn't know better I'd say you're afraid to leave me here with your friends." Todd glanced back toward the office where Gracie was. "I guess you're right, bad things could happen."

The bell over the door rang and he released her. It was Evan.

"Jenny?"

She put on a smile and moved away when her brother released her. "Evan."

He came over to her. "Is there a problem?"

Todd turned to face him. They were much the same size, Evan a little taller.

"I just came by to see my little sister," Todd said, holding out his hand. "Todd Newsome."

Evan took his hand and shook it. "Evan Rafferty."

"I'd like to stay, sis, but I need to get back to work. See you around, Rafferty."

Evan didn't like this guy at all. "Count on it, Newsome."

Todd paused, then walked out the door.

Evan went to the front of the shop and watched as Newsome got into an old pickup and drove off. He noted the license plate. He pulled out his cell phone and punched in Casali's number. He turned away and told him about Newsome's visit to the shop. After Alex suggested they meet with the sheriff, he hung up.

He turned toward Jenny. "Your leaving town has

nothing to do with a job, does it? It's your brother, isn't it."

She started to speak, but he stopped her. "Save it for when the deputy and Alex gets here. Now, where is Gracie?"

"She's in the office."

"Did Newsome threaten you or Gracie?"

She shook her head. "You'll be fine when I leave."

He couldn't stand to see the fear in her eyes. He had to make sure this guy was gone from her life. For good.

Over the next thirty minutes, Evan watched Jenny keep busy while Gracie did homework upstairs in her apartment.

She hadn't said much to him since her step-brother had left. He had trouble remembering the open, caring woman he'd made love to just the other night. Jenny was withdrawn and silent as she counted the day's receipts.

Okay, she was angry with his high-handedness, but he didn't care, he'd do anything to keep her safe. He couldn't lose her, not now.

"Jenny, this isn't your fault."

"Don't, Evan. We can't do this." She looked close to tears. "I don't want you involved in my mess."

"Newsome is causing the trouble, not you."

She shook her head. "Everyone says that. But even as a kid, he kept getting away with things." Those brown eyes showed fear. "I had reason to be afraid. You have no idea. Todd's mean. Cruel. When he was sent to prison, I was so relieved. I thought I was finally free of him. But he's back, and I can't let him hurt you or Gracie."

"What about you, Jenny? Who's going to worry about you?"

She shook her head. "I'll be fine, but Todd will find a way to get even with anyone who crosses him. I can't bear it if that's you. So I have to go."

Finally, Alex and Allison arrived through the back door, along with Deputy Reynolds. Once the shop was locked up tight, the meeting began to find out Newsome's agenda.

Alex got straight to the point. "Jenny, you should have come to us when your brother first threatened you."

Ashamed, Jenny shook her head. "I swear I didn't know he was responsible for the break-ins until yesterday. He still didn't admit it to me, but he didn't deny it, either. I'm sorry he did so much damage to the place." She looked at Evan. "That he hurt you."

Evan couldn't stand it. "Don't you dare apologize for that bastard. If you had been here alone…"

He marched across the room, too frustrated to go on.

Jenny suddenly felt everything crashing down. Evan had to hate her now.

"We still need to find proof," Alex said.

She shook her head. "Todd's too clever to get caught. Besides, if I go back to San Antonio he'll leave you all alone."

"And he'll prey on someone else," the deputy said. "I've learned more about Newsome. He's made the rounds for jobs. After the A Bar A turned him down, he went out to the Merrick Ranch. But the Merricks keep close tabs on the men who work for them." The deputy looked at Evan. "But Newsome does have a job. He works at the Roadhouse Club."

Jenny couldn't believe it. "They hired him?"

The deputy said, "I'm not sure how well you know the Roadhouse's reputation, but the place has been rumored to be connected to prostitution, drug trafficking. The past few months, there's been a federal undercover investigation. That's how I learned about Newsome's job as a dish-washer/bouncer. But your stepbrother's employment satisfied his parole officer."

Allison walked over to her friend. "You should have come to us when he first started making trouble."

The deputy said, "We'll do everything we can to protect you, Jenny. I don't think any of the rest of you are in danger since it seems Newsome found another game at the Roadhouse. From what I hear, he's running a credit-card scam."

"Can't you pick him up for that?" Jenny asked.

"We need proof, and since the feds are involved, we have to follow their lead," the deputy said. "It does seem your stepbrother is playing with a heavy hitter, the owner, Cesar Sanchez. That's who the feds want to get their hands on." He glanced around at the group. "One thing that is imperative is that we keep this information to ourselves for now. We can't let on to Newsome."

"Oh, God, I'm sorry, Alex, Allison," Jenny said, shaking all over. "I never meant to endanger your family."

"What about you, Jenny?" Allison began, looking angry. "You're family, too, and you need the most protection."

"That's why I have to leave. If I'm not around maybe he'll stay away from the people I care about."

The deputy spoke again. "I doubt that now. Newsome is in a brand-new ball game. We're hoping we get something on him so he'll go back to prison."

Jenny swallowed. "How can I help?"

Reynolds glanced at Alex. "Stay so we can protect you, and maybe your stepbrother will slip up."

Jenny wanted to feel relieved, hearing that maybe she'd be free of Todd. She stole another glance at Evan. But it was already too late, she'd probably lose the most important thing in her life. The man she loved.

CHAPTER THIRTEEN

THE last thing Evan wanted to do was leave Jenny alone at her apartment. They had to act normal so Newsome wouldn't become suspicious, but he wasn't going anywhere.

Jenny wasn't going to like that, but too bad. He wasn't about to let anything happen to her. And why not have Newsome think there was something going on between them? Maybe the guy would keep his distance.

After everyone left and he sent Gracie home with Matt, Evan knew that next he had to deal with Jenny's stubborn independence. After he locked the door and punched in the security code he followed her upstairs.

"I told you, Evan, I don't want you involved in my problems. If something were to happen to you…" She closed her eyes. "You need to think about Gracie."

"I *am* thinking about my daughter. I don't want scum like Newsome out there preying on innocent people. That's why he needs to be stopped—for good."

Jenny couldn't say any more as she turned away. All she knew was she had to keep her distance from Evan Rafferty. She couldn't let him see her true feelings. That was her only protection.

"What did he do to you?" Evan asked as he came up behind her.

She shook her head. "I don't want to talk about him. It's in the past."

"Not anymore." He frowned at her, his fists clenched. "Did he touch you? I'll kill him if he laid one finger on you."

She swung around to face him. "No!" she breathed. "Not that way. He pushed me around a few times, but I learned quickly to stay out of his way."

"What about your mother?" he asked. "Why didn't she help you? You're her daughter, for Christ's sake."

"She did as much as she could. But it didn't help with her marriage, either. She wanted to keep the family together."

"Dammit, Jenny. You shouldn't have to live like that, then or now."

He drew her into his arms and Jenny found she was too weak to resist this man. It was nice to lean on someone else…for a little while.

"I left. I worked for a scholarship and went away to college. I decided then that I wouldn't go back to that house."

"We'll get Newsome out of your life." His arms tightened around her, and she could almost believe him. "I promise."

She'd heard promises before. Did he mean they would be together? Suddenly, reality hit when a ringing sound caused her to jump. She took out her cell phone.

"Hello," she answered.

"Hey, sis. Did you have a nice evening with your friends?"

Hearing her brother's voice, she swallowed back the fear. Was he watching her?

"I take it Mr. Wonderful is there with you now. Is he spending the night? How cozy."

"It's my business what I do."

"Well, I'll be making it mine."

"Just leave me alone."

"Now is that any way to talk?"

She stole a glance at Evan. "I don't care whether you like it or not, not after you trashed my apartment and broke into the pawn shop."

"You better stop accusing me of things you have no proof of."

"Maybe I do have proof. Maybe I'll go to the sheriff with it, too."

Evan didn't look happy. But before Todd could say anything else, she yelled, "Stay out of my life." She closed her phone and discovered she was shaking. She glanced at Evan, not having to say who had been on the phone.

"You okay?"

She felt everything but. "Yeah, I feel great." She turned, walked into her bedroom and closed the door, shutting out everything she'd always wanted.

Hours later, Jenny still hadn't fallen asleep. She got up and went to the small window in her bedroom, feeling claustrophobic. She drew a tired breath, thinking about Evan sleeping in the other room. Just last week he'd spent the night in here with her.

She closed her eyes recalling their time together. How he'd made love to her body and her soul. How special he'd made her feel. As if she was the most precious woman in the world. A shiver went through her and she pushed it aside. She couldn't let herself get wrapped up in foolish dreams.

She had to survive this. To do what she needed to do, to have faith in law enforcement to handle her stepbrother and catch him in the act. But that might not happen, either.

If Todd was staying in Kerry Springs, harassing

her and her friends, her only choice was to leave. It was the best way to protect them.

That meant she had to leave a man she loved and a child she adored. There wasn't any other choice.

Jenny drew a shaky breath, walked across the bedroom and opened the door. She crossed the living area, opened the refrigerator and pulled out a bottle of water. After a long drink, she stole a glance at Evan sleeping on the sofa. With the streetlight coming through the window, she could see the outline of his body. She ached to go to him and let him help her forget. To pretend that everything was fine.

She closed her eyes. Why did this have to happen?

She started to leave the kitchen when he spoke. "Jenny? Are you all right?"

His words brought a smile to her lips. *No, I'll never be all right again.* "I was thirsty. Sorry I woke you."

He sat up. She saw his bare chest in the shadowed light. "I wasn't asleep."

"That's why you should have gone home."

He stood and came to her. She felt the familiar pull that she'd felt at their first meeting. "I want to be here."

She had to keep him away. "Oh, Evan. You don't want to get involved in my mess. It isn't safe."

"Not for you either," he pointed out. "We need to protect you from him."

"I think Todd got what he wanted, to scare me. Make sure I stay in line."

She shook her head. "Let's talk about something else." She leaned against the counter. "I hope you let Gracie keep coming to class."

He shrugged. "I doubt she will if you're not there."

She hated that. "She's pretty determined to finish her mother's quilt, so please, don't let her give up on it."

Jenny looked up at him. Even in the dim light he could see her eyes filled with tears. When she spoke, her voice was shaky. "She needs that closure…and so do you."

He liked that she was worried about everyone. "I closed that chapter with Megan a long time ago. We weren't the perfect couple, not even close." He hated talking about his failed marriage. "Maybe it was my fault, but you need two people in love to make it work. Megan and I were never in love. Gracie was the only reason we tried to stay together." He stole a glance at her. "When I met you, I realized how lonely I'd been for years. Even then I tried to fight it. But it was impossible not to care for you."

He didn't move toward her. "I think you care about me, too."

Jenny felt the deep longing in her chest, but fear held her back. "No, Rafferty. Of course not. Why would I care about you? You're not handsome or appealing at all. And your daughter…she isn't precious either. Just for the record, Megan was a fool."

When he grinned, she about lost it.

"Do you realize that you call me Rafferty when you try to put distance between us?"

"No, I call you Rafferty to make a point." Why was he so stubborn? "I can take care of myself."

He reached for her and pulled her against him. His warmth and strong arms felt so incredible.

"How's that working for you, Collins?" he began. "Now, listen to me. No matter what, you aren't going to run me off. I'm here for you."

She sighed, not wanting to hope. "Neither one of us needs this complication."

"You're wrong, Jenny, I need you," he said those simple words, and suddenly she realized that she needed him, too.

His head dipped and he took a gentle nibble from her lip. "So stop trying to get rid of me."

When his mouth closed over hers, her arms went around his neck. He kissed her in a way that made her believe. He was hungry and giving at the same time. He cupped her face and angled her head to give him better access and she went willingly.

Maybe they didn't have forever, but she could pretend for tonight.

The next morning Jenny awoke and found herself alone. She sat up on the sofa and glanced around the apartment, but there was no sign of Evan. It saddened her. He'd already broken his promise.

She ran her hand over her hair and walked into the kitchen. Coffee was made. Okay, that was a nice gesture. There was also a note.

Jenny,
You were sleeping and I didn't want to wake you. I went home to get Gracie off to school. I let the deputy know so he'd watch out for you. I'll be back,
Evan.

Her heart skipped a beat. Why did this man keep giving her hope? Hope for a future together. Last night they'd made love again, and afterward, he held her during the early hours of the morning.

She went to the phone and made the call to her school principal, Marge Burns, in San Antonio. She let her know that she couldn't take the summer-school position, but still wanted her regular job back for the fall session. Marge was fine with the change in plans.

After she hung up, guilt hit her. Okay, so she was still covering her bases in case everything fell apart. She couldn't expect Evan to offer her anything permanent. But this time, she wasn't settling for anything less.

An hour later, Evan drove Gracie to school. He wasn't taking any chances with Newsome out there. He needed to get back to Jenny. He could still feel the imprint of her body against his. He'd never felt such closeness with anyone before. She'd trusted him and fallen asleep in his arms. He pushed aside his doubts about himself, his insecurities about trying another relationship. About trusting someone again. He knew these same feelings were hard for Jenny, too.

He climbed out of the truck, kissed Gracie goodbye and watched until she went inside. He glanced around the parking lot, but didn't see anyone suspicious. He spotted Alex Casali's truck as he dropped off Cherry.

Evan went over to him and Alex asked, "Hey, how'd it go last night?"

"It was quiet," Evan said. "No sign of Newsome."

Alex studied him for a second. "It's good you were there for Jenny."

Evan wasn't sure he was ready to talk about this, but he'd thought about nothing else. "I'd like to be there more, but I'm not exactly in a perfect place right now." He still was in debt. "I'm not sure I can ask someone to take on a ready-made family."

Alex pushed his hat back and leaned against his truck.

"I've learned the past few years that with the right woman things just seem to work out. That is, if you love her."

Evan thought about the joy and happiness Jenny brought to him. "That's the easy part."

"What's the hard part?"

"Offering her a future. I have plans, but I'm not even close to reaching them."

Casali glanced off, and then back at him. "I'm always looking for a good, solid investment, and I hear Texas hill-country wine is just that. The thing is, though, I would need someone with expertise in the business. I would need a partner."

Two days later, on Saturday, Jenny moved around the class area at the shop trying to act as if everything was normal. But Todd's threats still had her on edge. Why did he have to ruin this for her? Okay, she'd talked about leaving, but, as of late, she wanted to make a home here. Permanently. In the one place that had ever felt like home.

Her thoughts turned to Evan. Finally she'd found what she'd been looking for, and yet, it was slipping through her fingers. She was high-risk now. When he'd returned the other morning, she let him know that he couldn't hang around her. He had to think about Gracie.

He wasn't happy about the idea, but finally he'd agreed to go along with it since Alex had hired around-the-clock security.

"Jenny," a tiny voice called to her.

She quickly came back to the present and the class as she glanced down at Gracie. "What, sweetie?"

The girl held up her sewn blocks of fabric. "How did I do?"

Jenny put on a smile and examined the stitches. "This is great. You've really improved."

Gracie smiled proudly. "I've been practicing at home. Daddy took out Mommy's sewing machine and helped me."

"Well, it shows." Jenny wasn't surprised. Evan had been growing closer to his daughter the past month. That was the best thing to happen out of this.

Looking at the clock, she saw it was nearly three o'clock. Her heart swelled as she watched the students working closely with their mentors. She'd enjoyed this class so much and she would miss it.

"You should be proud of this class."

Jenny turned around to see Lily Perry, who'd come to the class today, filling in for her mother, Beth Staley. "Coming from a principal that means a lot, thank you."

"This project has turned out to be a great idea. I believe there will be a long waiting list for the class next year."

"The volunteers have been wonderful."

"It's you the girls relate to. I wish I had your enthusiasm in my school." Lily smiled. "You wouldn't think about taking a position at the elementary level, would you?"

Jenny couldn't have been more surprised. "You're kidding, right?"

Lily raised an eyebrow. "If you're interested, call my office and we'll talk." She walked away.

Jenny cursed Todd again. She wanted this life, in this town. For the first time she'd let herself get involved, get attached to people: the Casalis, the Raffertys, even her job at the shop and the girls in her class. There were so many things she'd miss if she had to leave.

She thought about Evan and their night together. Her heart took a tumble and her breathing grew difficult. She wanted a lifetime of those nights in his arms. Did she dare to go after her dream?

At five o'clock, Jenny was about to close up for the weekend, but before she could bolt the front door, a dark figure came out of nowhere and pushed it open. Startled, she gasped as Todd forced his way inside.

"Get out!"

He ignored her and locked the door. "I'll leave when I'm ready." He grabbed her by the arm and pulled her away from the windows. "We need to have a little talk first."

She refused to let him bully her. There was a security guard out back. Surely he would check on her. "We have nothing to say."

"I'll decide that." He tightened his grip and jerked her toward the back.

"Stop it, you're hurting me."

"It will only get worse if you don't tell me what I need to know. Who's been following me?"

It was probably the authorities. "I don't know," she said.

"It's your boyfriend and his brother. They've been hanging out at the bar every night. Get them to back off or my boss will make them go away. Permanently."

Evan had been at the Roadhouse? What were

they trying to do? Whatever it was, it was too dangerous. "I have no control over what they do. We broke up."

"Well, he hasn't got the message. So let him know I mean business."

"You brought this on yourself when you broke into the shop."

He glanced toward the windows. "Serves you right after you wouldn't help me."

"You did break in."

He shrugged. "What's the big deal? Your rich friend replaced everything."

"What about the pawn shop? The owner can't afford the loss."

"Too bad. Now I need you to help me get out of town. Where's the money from today?" He tried to open the register.

She refused to give him anything more. "It's been deposited already."

He came back to her. She refused to show fear. "Why don't I believe you?"

"I don't care." She worked to keep the quiver out of her voice. "I'm not going to let you walk out of here with anything else."

"You'll do whatever I tell you to do if you want to get rid of me." His grip tightened. "Hand over the money."

He twisted her arm until she cried out. "Okay,

I'll give you the money." She pulled away and bent down under the counter to grab the canvas bag. That was when she saw the panic button that Alex had installed last week. She pushed it and grabbed the depository bag.

"Here." She tossed it at him. "I just want you to go far away. Pretend I never knew you or your brothers."

He grabbed a bunch of her hair. "You're an uppity bitch. You think you can talk to me like that?" He threw her up against the counter. "You never gave me any respect. You always thought you were too good for me."

"I was a kid." She braced her hands on the countertop. She had to fight him. "You always were a bully." She realized she needed to keep him here. "Always knocking women around."

He pressed his body against hers. "Yeah, and you like it a little rough, don't you? It adds that extra excitement."

She could barely breathe. *Dear God. Please, someone come and help me.* "Let me go."

"Come on, you can ask me nicer than that." He pulled her head back farther, so that she was nearly flat on the counter.

When he raised his hand she was ready and jammed her knee into his groin. With a cry, he released his hold on her and doubled over.

She had her chance and rolled away, putting the counter between them. "Get out. Now!"

He tried to straighten, wincing in pain. "You're not getting away with this." He caught up with her as she ran for the back door.

"Just leave. You got your money."

He pulled her arm behind her back and pushed her down on the fabric-cutting table. Then the first hit came, and she groaned with the pain. Stars appeared with the second strike and she worked to hold on to consciousness. She felt around and found the pair of scissors on the counter. The last thing she remembered was raising her arm and jamming them as hard as she could into her attacker. As Todd let out a cry, everything faded to black.

CHAPTER FOURTEEN

EVAN parked his truck in the alley. He wasn't going to wait any longer to see Jenny. He'd just finished up his meeting with Alex, and they'd tentatively agreed on a partnership for the vineyard. It was a big step and he wanted to talk it over with Jenny. More importantly, he needed to tell her of his true feelings—that he loved her.

He climbed out of the cab and was greeted by the security guard. With a nod to the off-duty officer, Jerry Regan, he headed for the back door.

"Jenny still working?" he asked.

"As far as I know." The guard's radio went off. "Regan here."

The dispatcher reported, "A code 7 in progress at your location. Repeat, code 7. Backup en route."

Evan worked to stay calm. "What does that mean?"

"The panic alarm went off."

Even rushed to the door, but it was locked. He pulled out the key he still had from the other night and opened it. Before the guard caught up, he was inside the shop where he saw Newsome leaning over Jenny on the table, his fist raised. Before Evan got to them, Todd slumped and fell on her.

With a throaty growl, Evan grabbed Todd's shirt and jerked him off her. That was when he saw the blood. Everywhere. The assailant groaned and was barely conscious as he slid to the floor.

Evan gasped for air as he looked down at Jenny, searching for any puncture wounds on her. There were none. Then he saw the rise and fall of her chest. She was alive.

"Oh, God, Jenny. I'm sorry." Tears flooded his eyes. He should have been with her. "Come back to me, honey. Open those beautiful brown eyes."

She finally stirred. With a moan, she blinked up at him. Her jaw was already starting to swell and one eye was red. "Evan…"

He gathered her gently into his arms. "I'm here, Jenny. I'm here. I'll always be here, so you'd better get used to it."

It had been two hours since the paramedics had worked on Jenny and brought her the hospital. Evan was still pacing the waiting room, desperate for news. He wouldn't be able to calm down until he heard that Jenny was okay.

The double doors opened and Alex and Allison rushed in. "How is she?"

"No word yet." Evan cursed under his breath. "It's a good thing that Newsome is hospitalized or I'd make sure he was."

Allison put her hand on Evan's arm. "The authorities will handle this." She offered him a smile. "I'm so proud of Jenny. She defended herself against that maniac."

Evan shook his head. "She wouldn't have had to if I hadn't left her by herself."

"You couldn't be with her every minute," Allison said. "She wouldn't have allowed that. And we all know how stubborn she can be."

"Too stubborn for her own good."

"Yeah, that's one of the reasons you love her."

Before he could respond, his father, brother and Gracie came bursting through the doors. His daughter was carrying flowers. He was suddenly glad they were all there.

"Daddy, Jenny's not going to die, is she?"

He didn't miss the panic in his little girl's eyes. She had to remember her mother being here. He gathered her into his arms. "No, sweetheart. She was awake when she was brought in. The doctor just wants to check her out to make sure everything is okay."

Gracie looked up at him. "Did they put that mean man in jail?"

Newsome's wound was pretty deep but not life-threatening and it wouldn't stop him from going to jail. "They will, and he's not going to hurt anyone ever again. We're going to make sure of that," Evan said, then walked away from the group, but his father followed him.

"Son, you can't blame yourself for any of this."

"I should have been there. She made me go away so we'd all be safe, but no one was there for Jenny. No one has ever been there for Jenny."

Tears filled Sean Rafferty's eyes. "You're here now."

That gave Evan little consolation as the doctor came down the hall toward him. "Are you Evan Rafferty?"

"Yes, I am. How's Jenny?"

The older man nodded. "She's doing fine. We did a scan and everything looks good. She has a slight concussion, and some facial bruising that will look worse by tomorrow, but no permanent damage or scarring."

Evan sighed with relief. "Can I see her?"

"She asked me to tell you she isn't up to seeing anyone right now."

He felt the hurt deep in his chest. "We won't stay long," he promised.

"I'm sorry," the doctor said. "I think she's self-conscious about the bruises."

"I don't care about the damn bruises," Evan hissed. "I just need to see that she's okay."

Allison came up behind him. "Evan, Jenny's been through a lot, she needs rest." She looked at the doctor. "Are you keeping her overnight?"

"We'd like to, especially since she doesn't have any family to look after her."

Evan raised his head, scared that he wouldn't be able to let Jenny know how he felt about her. "You're wrong. We're her family."

Evan had given Jenny three days. He still called, but she'd refused to talk to him. If he'd learned one thing from his first marriage, it was that he needed to let Jenny know his feelings. And dammit, one way or another he was going to talk to her today.

He glanced across the truck cab to where Matt sat. "You didn't have to come with me." He had no clue as to where Jenny had disappeared to, so he was going to start with Alex and Allison.

"Are you kidding?" Matt said. "When she turns you down, I'm going to make my pitch to her."

Gracie poked her head over the seat. "We all want to see Jenny. She can't go away, Daddy. Please, you've got to make her stay so she can be my mommy."

"I'm going to do my best."

"We all will," Sean added from the back seat.

Evan drove through the A Bar A gate. "Great. This is all she needs, the whole Rafferty clan."

"That's right," his dad called. "Jenny needs all of us. She needs her family."

"You love Jenny, don't you, Daddy?" Gracie asked.

His chest tightened. "Yes, sweetie. I love her." That brought a smile to his little girl's face. "And I'm going to do everything I can to make her stay here with us."

He parked at the Casalis' back door. He shut off the engine and climbed out as Alex came out and down the porch steps.

Evan walked closer. "Look, Alex, I know your wife and Jenny are best friends. I also know you have your loyalties, but if I have to search every damn inch of this ranch to find her, I will."

A smile tugged at the corners of Casali's mouth. "It's about damn time you showed up."

Jenny was still a little sore, but was feeling better, physically anyway, with each passing day. It had been three days since her release from the hospital. She'd been staying out at one of the A Bar A cabins at Cherry's Camp for disabled kids. The summer season hadn't opened yet so Jenny had all the quiet and solitude she would ever need.

It was totally overrated. She missed everyone.

At least she didn't have Todd to worry about any longer. She'd had an early-morning visit from the deputy sheriff. They'd let her know the feds had raided the Roadhouse and busted the credit-card ring. She'd also learned that when Todd couldn't get hired on at a ranch, he went out to the Roadhouse for a drink, and had found another opportunity. They'd liked his…potential.

Within a few weeks her stepbrother was running the scam like an expert. When Todd suspected someone was following him, he'd come to her for money to get out of town and across the border to Mexico.

After his arrest, Todd wasn't volunteering any information to the authorities. The one thing she did know was that with her testimony, her stepbrother was definitely going back to prison. By the looks of the charges, he could be out of her life for good.

Sadness washed over her. Could she ever get over the shame of her stepbrother's actions in this town, and what he had tried to do to her friends? That was the reason for her latest decision to leave Kerry Springs. She drew a breath and released it, thinking of all the people she would miss. Especially the Raffertys. Soon Evan would move on and find someone else.

There was a knock on the door and for a moment she felt a surge of hope. Was it Evan?

She opened to door to find Allison. "How long are you planning on hiding out here?" her friend asked as she stepped into the large living area designed for family members to stay during the camp.

"Are you throwing me out?"

Allison glanced at the open suitcase. "It doesn't look like I need to." Her eyes widened. "You're leaving?"

"It seems to be the best answer for everyone. Evan doesn't need this mess in his life. He has Gracie and a new business to think about."

"And I bet right now you're the only thing on his mind." Allison raised her hand to stop Jenny's protest. "I see how that man looks at you. I've only seen that once before. Correct that, I see it every day when Alex looks at me. For heaven's sake, Jenny, the man loves you."

Jenny couldn't say anything. She wanted to believe that. Tears filled her eyes; she knew she'd made a mess of things.

"We both need to move on with our lives. Once I testify against Todd, I can think about my future." Teaching kids had always been what she'd wanted to do. She sure hoped it still was, because it had to fill a lot of empty places in her heart.

"Great speech, Jen," Allison said. "I just hope it makes you happy on those long, lonely days and nights to come." She hugged her friend, then walked to the door. "Please stop by the house to say goodbye to the kids."

Once Allison was gone, Jenny wiped away the tears. She wanted nothing more than to stay here, but if she didn't leave now, she wouldn't be able to.

She closed her suitcase and wheeled it across the hardwood floors. With one last glance around, she opened the cabin door, nearly running into the man she'd been trying to avoid.

"Evan!" Her gaze ate him up. His powerful presence. His handsome face and those killer blue eyes that she would see in her dreams for a lifetime. Her chest tightened and she had to look away for a second. "I didn't expect you."

He nodded at her suitcase, a grim look on his face. "Sneaking out of town without even a goodbye. What, no guts, Collins?"

She opened her mouth but couldn't lie. Not to this man. She loved him too much.

"I'm sorry, Evan, I thought it would be better to send you a note. I mean, after everything that happened. It would be easier for both of us."

"Are you talking about the jerk that beat you up? Or is this about us—you and me? Those nights I made love to you? Those times I shared my heart, my soul with you? I thought they meant something to you, too."

Tears welled in her eyes. "They did. I've never felt this way about anyone else."

He moved toward her. "Then please tell me why in God's name you're running away."

She opened her mouth and couldn't speak, then suddenly it all gushed out. "Because I love you, Rafferty, darn it. And I don't want any of this ugliness to touch you or your family. Are you happy now?"

A slow, easy grin appeared as he drew her close. "How about you leave out the 'darn it,' and just say 'I love you, Evan.'"

She stopped fighting her feelings. "I love you, Evan," she breathed.

"And I love you, too, Jenny," he whispered against her mouth, right before he kissed her. She wrapped her arms around his neck and held on, enjoying the rush of feelings. Evan loved her. If she was dreaming it was the most wonderful of all dreams.

She broke off the kiss. "No, Evan, think about this, about your family. It's not over with Todd.

I have to testify, probably next year. Everything will come out, all the ugliness."

"You honestly think that bothers me? I've survived worse. The Rafferty family has survived much worse. My mother taking off. Me having to marry because I got a girl pregnant."

"This is so much worse. Todd stole from this town."

"And *he's* going to pay for it. Not you. You're not going to pay for anything. He's out of our lives, Jenny. Don't let him hurt us anymore."

"I don't want him to."

"This time you won't be alone. I'll be there. All the Raffertys will be. Families stick together." He turned her around and pointed to Matt, Sean and Gracie in the distance, standing beside the truck. They waved at her.

She waved back. "Oh, Evan. They should come over."

"Not yet, because they promised I'd get first dibs to convince you to stay here and marry me. If I blow it, Matt gets second shot." He glared. "Yeah, like I'd let him near you."

Marry him? Evan wanted her to marry him? She started to giggle, unable to control her emotions, then the tears came.

Evan wiped them away as he searched her face. Had he pushed her too far, too fast? "I'm sorry,

Jenny, I've upset you. It's too soon, I understand. We can wait awhile so you can be sure."

She shook her head. "Oh, Evan. You want to marry me?"

He pulled back to see her face. "I love you, Jenny Collins. God, I never realized how much until I thought I might lose you. When I found you at the shop and saw the blood…"

She touched his jaw. "Ssshhh, it's okay, Evan. I'm safe now."

"I'll never forgive myself for not being there with you, protecting you."

She smiled. "You're here now."

"And if you let me, I'm going to make sure that I will always be here." He released a long breath. "I know my husband skills are a little rough, but I can change. I have changed since you've come into my life." He stared into her incredible brown eyes. "I don't want to live without you, Jenny. I need you. You're the perfect mother for Gracie. She loves you, too. Besides, you need to be around to help her finish her quilt." He pulled her closer. "And there's our future children that I want to have with you. Only you."

Children. Evan's children. This dream was getting better and better. "I love Gracie, too. And I love you, and your dad and your brother. Your entire family."

He worked up a frown. "Not as much as me, right?" he teased.

She looped her hands around his neck. "Never as much as you." She pressed her mouth against his and began to convince him of her words. It wasn't until they heard the sound of loud whistles that they broke apart.

He rested his forehead against hers. "Are you sure you can handle this much family?"

"As long as I have you, Rafferty."

"Always."

"Then bring 'em on."

Evan raised his arm and everyone came running toward them. Jenny was suddenly surrounded by kisses and hugs.

No, she could never have too much love and family.

EPILOGUE

THE past few months at the Blind Stitch had been busy, but happy times for Jenny. And today, Saturday, was her last day. She'd already started her new teaching position at the elementary school, and with the wedding next weekend, she had so much to finish.

It didn't mean she wasn't going to miss coming to the shop every day, seeing the customers. Jenny looked toward the table in the Quilters' Corner to see the familiar group. The ladies—Beth, Louisa, Liz and Millie, of course—had helped her through the past few rough months. She not only had a loving soon-to-be-husband and his family, but so many good friends in this town.

Since her own mother had learned that she would be testifying against Todd, she'd declared that she wanted nothing to do with her only daughter. That had hurt Jenny, but it had been Sean who'd wrapped her in a loving embrace and told her she was his daughter now. Also, the citizens of

Kerry Springs had banded together to support her, welcoming her into their community. She finally had a place where she fitted in.

And the shop was a special place for her. She went to the window where her class's quilt was draped over the stand on display. Each student had worked hard to finish her family blocks, and the end product had turned out to be very colorful.

Below it was the winning family essay, which had been won by Cherry Cole Casali. No one could compete with all the Casali family history, going back to Italy and England. Gracie was a little disappointed, but was happy for her friend. Jenny told her there was always next year.

Jenny turned away from the window and discovered the ladies smiling at her. Then she heard voices and glanced toward the back of the shop as Allison, carrying a large cake box, walked in followed by Cherry, Gracie and Alex and Evan.

Not that she didn't want to see her husband-to-be, but he usually didn't come into town these days. She realized they had planned some kind of party. She went and hugged Evan. "Okay, what's going on?"

"We just thought we'd stop by, seeing as it's your last day and all."

"Yeah, Jenny," Gracie said with a giggle. "We

thought you'd be sad today so we came by to cheer you up."

Jenny turned back to the table, where suddenly a large wrapped box had appeared on top.

She was embarrassed. "What's this?"

"It's a gift for the two of you," Beth said.

Jenny had trouble accepting presents. She glanced down at her square-cut diamond ring that Evan had slipped on her finger only weeks ago. He'd spent far too much on it, but she loved it. She glanced up at Evan then back at her friends.

"But you all had a bridal shower for me last month. You didn't need to get me another present."

"Okay, so it's your first wedding gift," Liz Parker said. "We wanted to give it to you here at the shop." She slid the box toward her. "It's something for you and that handsome bridegroom of yours."

"Open it, Jenny," Gracie coaxed her.

Caught up in the excitement, she tore at the wrapping, then lifted the lid to reveal her gift.

She covered her mouth to quiet her gasp as she stared down at the beautiful quilt, folded perfectly to show off the interlocking circles with the date of the approaching wedding embroidered in the center. The pattern was similar to the Twisted Rope design, but different. The pastel shades of blue, rose pink, spring green and cream were stunning together.

"Oh, my. Oh, my. This is absolutely gorgeous."

Allison stepped closer. "I hope we got your colors right."

Jenny took the large blanket from the box and the ladies helped spread it out. She turned to her friend. "This is one of your designs, isn't it?"

Her best friend shrugged as she leaned back against her husband. "I came out of retirement for a few months."

"We all helped," Gracie volunteered. "We even got some of your and daddy's material." She pointed to a familiar fabric. "See. This is Daddy's shirt." Jenny remembered the soft blue denim shirt.

"I donated your bathrobe," he whispered against her ear. "But I'll never forget how you looked in it."

Jenny blushed at the memory.

Allison nodded to the group of women. "I also had these talented ladies who refused to quit until the project was completed. They wanted it finished before the wedding."

"I love it."

"Can't wait for those cold nights," Evan added.

Jenny's blush grew worse. "We thank you all so much." She hugged her friend, feeling the sting of tears. She went around to everyone. "I've never had anything so beautiful."

"I learned a long time ago," Allison began, "that the best quilts aren't about fancy patterns. They're the ones that are made with love by the caring hands of friends. Ones that tell a story. Millie, Liz, Beth, Louisa, Lisa and Cherry and Gracie all wanted to make sure that you and Evan had your new beginning. The beginning to your family, for future generations of Raffertys.

"Starting with…" Allison pointed to the block where Gracie's name was stitched in one of the circles on a pink heart-print fabric. "She chose this material and she worked very hard at sewing her name."

"I practiced a lot," the child said.

"I bet you did." Jenny hugged her little girl, knowing she was getting a daughter along with a brother and a father with this marriage, which was more than she could ever have hoped for. She ran her fingers over the next circle with her and Evan's upcoming wedding date, then over the cream print stashing where each woman's initials were stitched.

Millie walked in carrying the cake. "You'll notice there's plenty of room for baby names," she said. "And the ladies of the Quilters' Corner will add them at no extra charge."

Jenny felt a warming in her heart. Evan and she had talked about babies. They both wanted children. Soon. "I'll treasure it always." She stole a look at the group's smiling faces. "Thank you. This is so special to me."

"You're special to us, too." Allison hugged her. "We wanted to make sure you knew that this town is your family, too."

"We do baby quilts, as well," Beth Staley said, and everyone laughed.

Jenny felt Evan's arms tighten around her, holding her close. "First, we're going to produce next year's vintage, then we'll have you working on those quilts."

Gracie added her request. "Daddy, can we have two, like Cherry's mom?"

Everyone laughed again as Evan drew his daughter into their embrace. "Maybe Jenny and I need to talk about it first." Evan winked at Gracie and gave her a smile. "But I'll do my best to convince her."

A week later, just after grape-harvest time in the Texas hill country, Evan knew he had so much more to be thankful for than just the bountiful harvest.

This was his wedding day. The beginning of his and Jenny's life together.

Standing on the rise, he looked over the vineyard at the rows of vines that lined the hillside. In a few short hours he would have Jenny to share all this with. Since the day she'd agreed to be his wife and mother to Gracie, everything had only gotten better for them.

"Hey, Rafferty. Are you having second thoughts?"

He turned around and saw his bride. His breath caught and his throat closed up. She was dressed in a long ivory gown of lace that draped over her slender body like a dream. She held up the dress's train as she made her way toward him. A white orchid was pinned in wheat-colored hair that had been pulled back from her pretty face.

He'd sent her a message that he wanted to see her alone before the ceremony, just an hour away. And she was here.

He couldn't find enough oxygen. "You're breathtaking."

She smiled. "That was the look I was going for."

Jenny was nervous and giddy at the same time. She gave her husband-to-be a long look. He was handsome in his Western-cut tux that emphasized his broad shoulders. He'd added shiny black boots that were the perfect touch.

"You don't clean up so bad yourself, Rafferty."

He took her hand in his. She loved the roughness of his palms as he walked her to the edge of the rise, then he leaned down and placed a gentle kiss on her mouth. Soon she'd forgotten about destroying her makeup, or that two hundred people were to arrive at the ranch in about an hour.

She pulled back. "What is so important that we're breaking tradition and you're seeing your bride before the wedding?"

He grinned mischievously and her heart tightened. She loved this man so much.

"I want to give you something before everything gets crazy today."

She sobered. "We didn't have to do a big wedding."

He shook his head. "No, we'll start this marriage out with good memories. I want everyone to see how much I love you and want us to have a life together."

"Oh, Evan, you don't have to prove anything to me." She looked up at him. "I know you love me." She took a breath. "We've all been so busy. So much has happened to us."

Evan's partnership with Alex Casali was the beginning of their future. Alex was building the winery on adjoining property he'd purchased a few months ago. Evan had already started interviewing vintners to handle the operation.

They looked down at the now-finished structure

that at one time was to be a winery he'd planned with Meg. Now it was going to be the Rafferty Family Vineyard's new tasting room. That way, when their label, Rafferty's Legacy, came out, it would be at home. The first vintage would be bottled in a few years at the Casali and Rafferty Winery.

She went on. "It's like a dream. You'll get to work at what you love, growing your grapes and now you have your label."

"It's *our* label, Jenny." He gripped both her hands as his blue eyes gazed into hers. "None of this matters unless you're with me."

Evan realized there were no truer words. He couldn't imagine his life without her in it. They each had their second chance.

"You're everything to me, Jenny." He shut his eyes. "In only a few short months, you've changed my life. My daughter's life."

"*Our* daughter's life," Jenny corrected. "I love her as if she were my own."

His heart tightened with emotion. He'd never known he could feel like this. "In a short time we'll be married right here in front of family and friends, but first, I needed to be with you, alone." He gripped her hand. "I want to give you something." He reached into his pocket and pulled out a platinum necklace with a heart covered with tiny diamonds and a sapphire in the center.

"Oh, Evan."

"I know it's not the one you lost, but I wanted you to know that you'll always have my love, my devotion and my heart."

She fought tears. "It's beautiful."

He fastened it around her neck and kissed her.

She touched the heart lovingly. "Perfect."

He took her hand. "It's time to begin our life together."

Jenny knew she'd never been so happy. Together they walked down the hill to greet their guests. She'd found her place with this man. She'd always known she could stand alone, but now she knew this was where she was meant to be. With Evan. Forever.

The series you love are now available in

LARGER PRINT!

The books are complete and unabridged—
printed in a larger type size to make it
easier on your eyes.

❖ Harlequin®
Romance

From the Heart, For the Heart

❖ Harlequin®
INTRIGUE®
BREATHTAKING ROMANTIC SUSPENSE

❖ Harlequin®
Presents~

Seduction and Passion Guaranteed!

❖ Harlequin®
Super Romance®

Exciting, emotional, unexpected!

Try **LARGER PRINT** today!

Visit: www.ReaderService.com
Call: 1-800-873-8635

❖ Harlequin®

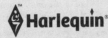

A *Romance* FOR EVERY MOOD™

www.ReaderService.com

HLPDIR11